The Man Who Loved Zoos

Malcolm Bosse

THE MAN
WHO LOVED
ZOOS

G. P. Putnam's Sons
New York

To friends

The Man Who Loved Zoos

1

With the long coat flapping around his ankles, he hunched into the steady wind that often sweeps before dawn through the San Francisco hills. Parked ahead of him on the otherwise empty street was a bus filled with passengers. He saw them at the windows, their heads leaning against the glass, dozing in the undersea gloom. Drawing nearer, he could see that not all were asleep: An old man was sneering down at him, teeth bared, and from the next window a fat woman was grinning, her mouth pulled mockingly to one side.

The young man raised his middle finger in an obscene gesture. Let people make fun of him for his beard and long coat; he would make fun of their conformity. So he shuffled alongside the bus until coming to its open door, where he turned and with a smile raised his finger higher. But there was no driver at the wheel to insult and no sound from within. He listened and then set his foot tentatively on the first step. What decided him finally to climb into the bus was the silence coming from it like a peculiar smell. He edged up the stairwell to the front of the aisle, next to a seated child whose head lay on a woman's shoulder. The whites of the boy's staring eyes seemed to glow in the half-light, and his small hand clutched the woman's thigh. When the young man bent over for a closer look, he saw that the boy was dead.

So were they all.

Slowly he walked up the aisle, squinting down at men and women of all ages, at a busload of ordinary people who weren't breathing. Here and there a hand was thrust out, a head thrown back, a body slumped over, but none of the people had set themselves for defense or escape. He turned at the rear of the bus and stroked his beard thoughtfully. He was used to death coming with violent struggle and often messily, but these corpses looked like people dozing on a long trip. He reached out and lightly ran his forefinger across the cheek of a middle-aged woman. Her skin was cold but still resilient. It was spooky. And the violet light of early morning, the motionless air within the bus, the total silence, all added to his sense of this happening in a dream. And yet he stood there only a few moments before starting to rifle through the clothes of the dead passengers. Working toward the front, he deposited rings, watches, traveler's checks, loose money, and wallets into the frayed pockets of his oversized coat. His hands moved nimbly through handbags and into trousers and jackets. A few times he paused at windows to see if anyone was coming, then went back to his systematic work. When his coat could hold no more, he stuffed his pockets, except the right front one that was ripped. To make room he threw out the worthless contents he had been carrying in them into the aisle: half of a pencil, a few Kleenexes, a Vicks inhaler, some throat lozenges, and a cheap spiral notebook whose cover was nearly torn off. When his pockets were crammed with money and jewelry, he loaded up his shirt pockets, then filled one of the women's handbags, and by the time he returned to the front of the aisle, he was weighed down by loot. After a single glance at the dead boy, he scrambled out of the bus and hurried away. Someone was approaching from the next block, so he turned downhill and scurried around the first corner. Had he been seen? It was hard to tell in the murky light, but someone in uniform had been coming toward the bus.

He ran until a stitch in his side brought him to a halt. Leaning against a wall, he worked to get his breath back. No one was following, but that had been a uniform coming toward the bus. He started to trot, this time uphill, everything jingling on him, metal against metal like a junkshop in motion. At the next corner he turned downhill, gasping for breath. The uniform wasn't following, so he stumbled into the dark recess of a storefront and leaned against the window, breathing hard. He stuffed the handbag inside his shirt and buttoned his coat, seeing as he did so a bunch of dollar bills sticking out between his fingers. In the niche of darkness he forgot the bus, the people, the uniform, and lived for a few anguishing moments in the memory of a friend's death. His friend had clutched some leaves and whimpered like a dog.

The uniform belonged to the bus driver who was returning from a phone call. Three sidewalk phones had been out of order, so he'd walked for blocks before finding one that worked. Then he got a bad connection. "That's the part I need," he shouted into the phone. "I can put it in in a jiffy, but—what's that? Talk louder! Yes, that's the part. I said, that's the part!" He squinted down the empty street, awash in blue light. "Listen, get here quick. I wasted time finding this goddamn phone. I'm about ten blocks away. Where?" He gave an address. "No, that's where the *bus* is. I'm ten— what? The bus is *there*, I'm ten blocks away!" A young couple was emerging from an apartment house. "Listen, I'm not sticking around here long. What? Okay, okay, don't worry, I'll wait." He watched the young couple hesitate, then set out in the opposite direction. "But get here quick.

Another hour," he said breathlessly, "we'll have a crowd ten deep and how am I gonna explain a busload of stiffs!"

The morning paper said nothing.

He waited for the evening edition, but it said nothing too.

He couldn't understand this: forty people dead on a bus and no mention of it in the news. He went into a bar and watched for it on TV, but they talked only of a drug raid and a cop gunned down on Market Street. No busload of dead people who looked as if they were on a long trip. Well, they sure were on a long trip, and it didn't matter to them whether the news advertised that fact. The dead people he had seen—and he'd seen plenty—never cared if you rolled them over with your boot or counted a dozen of them when there were half that many. Phony body counts and a news report didn't matter to them, because they stared up at you from a world of their own, indifferent to what you thought.

He finished his beer, watching on TV the Lions run a touchdown against the Bears.

And so the dead didn't care if you took their goods, either. Sniffling, he took out a Kleenex and blew his nose hard. With all that money he could impress the girl he had met a few days ago at the zoo in front of the Eurasian brown bears. She was one of those slick blondes who like to go places; on an hour's notice she would probably be ready for a wild weekend in Hawaii. He blew his nose again, deciding to call her. At the phone booth, however, he couldn't find the notebook with her number in it, and then remembered that he had thrown the old thing in the aisle to make room for goods. He used up three dimes on wrong numbers before he finally got her—or rather her answering service that told him she was out. She wouldn't be out if she knew that back in his room he had a drawerful of traveler's checks

4

and jewelry. Shoving the beer glass aside, he called for whiskey, an expensive Scotch.

The next morning he awoke with a bad hangover, that bus on his mind. Where had the driver been and why hadn't the news carried the story? He used to think that Vietnam was a dream and home a reality, only after getting out of the hospital he hadn't been so sure; maybe both were dreams, and reality was where the animals lived.

He reached over for a Kleenex, blew his nose, got up, and threw on pants and shirt. Barefoot, with toothbrush in hand, he left his room, locked it, and rushed down the hall to the bathroom. Thank God it wasn't occupied; he hated to stand out there waiting. He rinsed the stale whiskey taste from his mouth and then, sheepishly, unbuttoned his shirt and trousers. For a few moments he stared at the vicious zigzag scar that ran from his ribs to his groin, an angry red ridge of flesh that made his body look ugly and weak. Someone was pounding on the door, so he buttoned up quickly and left the bathroom without a glance for the person waiting.

It was time for him to leave for the zoo. He took a bus and arrived at the Fleishhacker before noon. Although the ocean breeze was crisp, the day was not chilly enough to warrant heavy clothing, so people stared at his ankle-length coat. Not that Warren gave a damn what they thought, but their eyes could make him feel uneasy. What were they looking for, a glimpse of the puckered scar? Not that it mattered, and to hell with people, because he was at the zoo now, where usually he could forget them. He strolled from exhibit to exhibit, his eyes fixed on the animals. He especially liked the long-armed gibbons looping from bar to bar, and the playful seals sliding through water with the ease of oil. Birds didn't interest him, they were too quick and noisy, and sometimes they appeared in his nightmares, but in the Reptile House he stood at the mamba cage, waiting until the emerald rope rippled. He saved the big cats for last, because it was in front of their cages that he had the fantasy. A fat leopard lay there on the cement with its yellow eyes half closed, dreaming of jungles. In the fantasy Warren climbed over the rail to the cage and opened its door. The cat blinked lazily for a while before understanding that the door was open; then, with an abrupt motion, the big body rose, flabby muscles bunching for a spring. Warren moved swiftly along the line of cages, opening doors for lions, pumas, tigers, and cheetahs. Then there was a blur of color—yellows and tans and blacks—all slipping away from the barred cages, out into the crowd and from there into the brilliant sunlight. As people scattered from their path, the big cats padded silently toward the ocean and hunkered at the cliff overlooking the blue water. In their eyes was reflected the hazy horizon on which a ship soon appeared and drew near. It was an amphibious craft, and when it reached the shore the bow lowered and the animals picked their way down the cliff into the bowels of the ship. Warren was at the helm and set his course for Africa.

People stared at the bearded young man in the overcoat that reached to his ankles. He was standing in front of the leopard cage, grinning wildly.

Victoria Welch was furious. Yesterday Miss Sackman had caught her in the stacks reading a little essay by Lafcadio Hearn, "When I Was a Flower," a charming thing about him bursting into bloom, and today she had been assigned the circulation desk instead of reference. "Are you getting that for a reader or are you reading it for yourself?" Sackman had asked. Old Sackman was a librarian who wouldn't read novels, bragged that she hadn't read one in five years because they lacked educational value. Sackman was a Cancer, born on July 3, the same date as Louis XI, who had invented a torture box for his political enemies. Each Saturday morning chief librarian Sackman inventoried her whole apartment, including the contents of her refrigerator. She wrote everything down in a list—two frozen chicken pot pies, a half jar of olives, three oranges, and so on. Sackman was a low Cancer, possessive and devious, with a cruel streak running behind her fixed smile.

Victoria Welch was having such grim thoughts when she noticed her nephew approaching the circulation desk. The big coat hung loosely on his small-boned frame, giving him the look of a little boy lost, except for the unruly black beard that emphasized the sad eyes of a grown man. Had he been drinking again?

He leaned toward her, grinning, and asked for a Kleenex.

"Another cold?" She reached under the desk and opened her bag. "Do you know why you have them?"

He took the Kleenex and blew his nose so loudly that a nearby reader turned and scowled.

"Because you're depressed," Victoria said. She was slightly shorter than he but a good fifty pounds heavier; her superior weight made it easier for her to scold him, and he needed scolding, having been out of the hospital for a month now. Half of his discharge pay had gone to an anti-war organization and the other half had gone into drink. Other boys had been to war and come home men. Why hadn't her nephew, who had been her ward since the age of twelve? What had she done wrong? She wanted to explain to him that his colds were psychosomatic, the result of an aimless life. She wanted to tell him that he needed a job and a girl, but when she looked at that terrible coat and shaggy hair and unkempt beard, all she could think of was the beautiful boy he had once been, running down the beach and clapping his hands until they were a blur of motion, and so she merely asked him where he had been today.

"The zoo," he said. "And guess—"

A reader was waiting to have a book checked out, so Victoria left him awhile. She hoped that old Sackman wouldn't come out of the office and see him and say something vicious: "Is that your *war* hero? Don't tell me he's taking out *books*. Or are you just chatting?"

Victoria went back to him, where he stood rubbing his red nose with the Kleenex.

He laughed and winked. "You won't believe this," he began and then told her a weird story about a bus, dead people, and what he had done.

"No," Victoria whispered, leaning toward him, "I won't believe it." Another reader called to her and she busied herself checking out a book. Her hands were trembling as she wondered if he had lost all sense of reality. Oh, why had her sister died and left her this awesome responsibility! She went back to him.

"It happened, Aunt," he said solemnly.

Her nephew had never been a liar, and even during the hospital experience and the aftermath, when he had spent most of his time prowling the zoo, Warren had been mentally competent. Could he *rob the dead?* She looked at his forlorn figure, draped in that long coat, and at his dark eyes burning with the inner fire of someone struggling with a way of life he didn't understand, and it came over her that Warren might very well do something inexplicable and shocking—in defiance of the world.

"If you did that," she told him in a low voice, "you better go to the police."

"Not me."

"They'll understand."

"Yeah? I've had enough government food to last a lifetime."

The back of her neck bristled, a familiar sensation. She turned slightly and saw old Sackman approaching from the office, a fixed smile on her round, bespectacled face.

"Here comes the Gestapo," Warren muttered, and turned on his heel, and shuffled away.

"Warren," Victoria called, loud enough to turn a reader's head, but he was gone. Poor Warren, she thought, a Pisces with his moon in Gemini, born February 28. Astrologically he was marked for trouble; first the terrible wound in Vietnam and now this bus incident. It was precisely the kind of scrape that a Pisces with his moon in Gemini would get into.

"Is your nephew taking out books these days?" began Miss Sackman and without waiting for a reply she said, "It's come to my attention that people are keeping handbags under the desk. We can't have that, Victoria. There's enough sloppiness in the library as it is."

In a neighborhood bar he waited for the evening news on TV. This time they did talk of a bus and showed pictures of one that had plunged from the Coast Road onto the tide-washed rocks below. When the camera zoomed in on the crumpled metal being hauled by crane from the water, Warren recognized the bus. The commentator announced that there were no survivors among the passengers who had been on a tour of the western states. There hadn't been any survivors, Warren thought, long before the bus had ended up on rocks below the Coast Road. Not that it mattered, because those people didn't give a damn anymore. He had seen things as peculiar: a shoe with a man's foot in it swaying like fruit from the top branch of a tree. When you've seen something like that, it's hard to get excited about anything again, except a good time and a pretty girl. He took out a Vicks inhaler and sniffed deeply. Those goods were his now and he could use them as he pleased. He went to the phone booth and called the blonde again, but again her answering service told him that she was out. He didn't leave his number, afraid that she wouldn't call him back. After all, it had only been a chance encounter in front of the Eurasian brown bears. She hadn't even liked animals, but had simply gone to the zoo out of restlessness. She giggled at his enthusiasm—he noticed that—and refused his invitation for a beer, even though she gave him her phone number. "I think I'm too expensive for you," she said with a laugh. Her name was Julie and she looked like Louise, a girl he had made love to on the beach during high school days, before a Vietcong mortar had shattered his body and left him weak and ugly.

Warren got drunk. He remembered reciting the Boy Scout oath and telling someone, "There are more things in heaven and earth than are dreamt of in your philosophy, Horatio." He almost got into a fight about his coat. "It's nobody's business if I wear it," he shouted. "I do what I damn please. I go where I want, and nobody's going to stop me." Back in his room in the sleazy North Beach hotel, he sprawled on the bed and wondered where he'd like to go, now that he had money. Abruptly he got out of bed and went to the hall phone. Soon he heard his aunt's sleepy voice.

"I'm leaving for San Diego tomorrow," he told her.

"Warren, have you been drinking?"

"I'm going to the zoo there. It's the biggest in the world."

"You must stop *drinking*."

"There's something I want you to do for me, Aunt. Will you do it?"

"What is it?"

"I'll come by in the morning."

He hung up and went back to his room. Good old Aunt Victoria had always stood by him and he loved her, the only person in the world who cared if he lived or died. She had feelings and no wonder men had asked her to marry them, even though her eyes were too small, her nose too big, her body too chubby, like a rumpled koala bear. Warren flung himself on the bed, lights whizzing under his eyelids, his body numb from whiskey. But in all of her sixty years, Aunt Victoria had never learned that there was only one rule to live by, a bright, cold, bitter principle of life that you learned best in war: Take what you can get and to hell with everything else.

He had money now and the desire to see the greatest zoo in the world and nothing else mattered, not even Julie who had only laughed at him. Warren put some Privine drops up his nostrils and after a while fell asleep, his final waking thoughts of the big cats blinking from their cages and of the dead boy staring up from another world in that dark and silent bus.

2

In the small but elegant gallery the art dealer Alexander Boyle was showing new paintings to a wealthy collector. Alexander Boyle was tall, broad-shouldered, with thinning brown hair and the kind of face that adjusts to any scene— the opera or golf course or hardware store. In his dark suit he looked now like a salesman of expensive goods, and his low-pitched voice was having its effect upon the client. In ten years Alexander Boyle had made a success of the gallery, coupling a flair for discovering artists with a talent for selling their work. His pleasure in this achievement was tinged with sadness, because his wife hadn't lived to see her prediction come true. For most of their married life she had urged him to give up his dangerous profession and make his hobby a full-time occupation. Perhaps he would have continued to resist her arguments if the terminal disease had not begun to cripple her and had not awakened in him the desire to please. He understood now that a man could change his life successfully in middle age, and he was wistfully grateful to Cora for having exacted a promise from him on her deathbed to attempt such a change. It was not, however, altogether that simple. There were times when

12

the old life still called out to him, bullying him to accept an assignment. When a man has lived on the precipitous edge for most of his adult life, the need for total commitment reasserts itself in him with the urgency of an addiction. For more than a year Alexander Boyle had enjoyed a quiet existence. So a few days ago, when Hirschorn called, he had been ready, like a fruit ripening on a bough.

His assistant came into the gallery and called him aside, telling him that Mr. Hirschorn had called again. Boyle nodded, went smiling back to his client, and within ten minutes closed the deal. Then he told his assistant he would take a long lunch today. Leaving the gallery he had a last envious glimpse of skinny Mr. Vertrees whose fingers were often sticky from chocolate. Young men could eat what they pleased, and that thought depressed him.

In a Nob Hill restaurant he ordered plain tuna fish and a green salad, neither of which he liked. As recently as a month ago he had pleased the captain by ordering quiche Lorraine and other French specialties featuring cream sauces, butter, and richly marbled meat. Cholesterol, not vanity, had forced on him this new regimen. He was carrying around more than five hundred milligrams of fat in each cubic centimeter of his blood, his lipid count was extremely high, too, and according to the doctor, this was like holding a loaded pistol to his heart. So now the captain took his order with a disdainful smirk, and when the tuna fish came, Alexander Boyle ate it with the grim resolution of a small boy who would rather have hamburger.

Finished, he patted his slight paunch self-righteously, and went to the phone booth. A secretary put him through to the realtor Allen Hirschorn.

"Yes, Mr. Boyle, thank you for calling." The voice was cheery but formal, the impersonal voice of a cautious businessman. "There's some difficulty with the property we discussed. Can I call you, say, in ten minutes?"

Boyle gave him the restaurant number, went back to a

cup of Sanka, without a cigarette to make it palatable, and waited until Hirschorn called from somewhere out of the office.

This time when Boyle went to the phone booth, the voice he heard was tense, familiar.

"Alex, somebody got to those people and robbed them before the bus went over the cliff."

Boyle whistled between his teeth, staring irrelevantly at a chocolate mousse passing by from the kitchen.

Hirschorn explained that a Bay Area police chief had identified the dead from a passenger list, because their bodies had been cleaned of wallets and other valuables. Had the looting been done *after* the accident, it would have required blowtorches, a heavy crane, and hours of work in such wreckage, especially with the bus half submerged in water. Since the ransacking had been done *before* the accident occurred, it was obviously a planned heist.

"Is he investigating?" asked Boyle.

"You know these cops. He called in the FBI."

Boyle knew them all right. The Bay Area police chief must have been damn glad that the tour bus had crossed state lines, so he could call in the bureau. What had happened was simple enough for a good cop to understand: A few hoods had planned a bus robbery. Probably they had followed the bus in a pickup truck, stopped it on a lonely stretch of road, robbed the passengers, then sent the bus over the cliff with a push from the truck. Something like that had taken place a few years ago south of Big Sur. What must have bothered the police chief was not the viciousness of the crime but its professionalism. To track down such criminals would take time, and he probably had his hands full keeping peace in a town harboring dope pushers and racial tension. Let the bureau take the responsibility for a job that would drain energy he could employ better elsewhere. He must have been oilily cooperative, welcoming the chance to stay out of it.

14

"So what's the bureau doing?"

"I know this much—they're not telling the press anything. As far as the public's concerned, it's an accident."

"Yes, but what about the missing property?"

"That's the catch. If it was an *accident,* all that stuff should be recoverable."

"But it wasn't worth much."

"But it was *personal* stuff, Alex. Some of those next of kin are going to want it back."

Good solid citizens who would want back the mementos of their loved ones. Boyle could imagine some of them becoming insistent, and a few of them going so far as to prod a reporter or two into action.

"Goddamit," said Boyle.

"Now who in the hell robbed them, Alex? That's the problem now."

"It sure is a loose end."

"It's worse than a loose end. I've been wondering—what about your driver?"

"He's always been reliable," Boyle answered immediately. "I've worked with him for years."

"Better check him out."

"I will, I'm meeting him for payment later today."

"For *complete* payment?"

Boyle hesitated. "Complete payment comes tonight," he said.

"If it wasn't him, then who?"

"What about people on your side?"

"Not a chance."

Boyle was watching through the glass door of the booth all the sumptuous dishes passing by on tray after tray, but his thoughts had returned to that wind-swept night, the empty street, the bus silent as the tomb it actually was, those faces emerging slowly in the first light like fish from the depths of the sea. "Wait a minute," he said abruptly. "Remember I told you the bus broke down and my driver left it to phone me? While he was gone, somebody could have climbed in. There was time."

"Okay, but when you brought him the fuel hose, didn't you *check* the inside of the bus?"

"Maybe my driver checked."

"Yes, but you should have, too. I thought you had."

Boyle knew he should have: A man could be forgiven an error in judgment, but not a lapse in procedure. "Well," he sighed, "what now?"

"It's obvious, Alex. You better get that missing property back."

"Goddamit."

"I know. We worked out a good operation, considering the haste."

"But I should have checked the bus," Boyle admitted, almost adding, "this is what happens when you don't work full time. You get amateurish."

It was blustery down by the Oakland docks. Gulls were squawking overhead, and in the distance a ship's winch was humming gutturally. He caught a whiff of cinnamon in the air and for an instant thought of his wife, who used to make cinnamon toast every Sunday. Refrigeration trucks, jammed bumper to bumper, were bound for the piers. Scraps of brown wrapping paper, oily from fish, eddied about his feet as he turned into a waterfront saloon. When he entered the dimly lit place, a number of stevedores clumped together at the near end of the bar turned slightly to study him. He walked past them with the rolling gait of an ex-boxer and in his dark suit he looked like a gangster stopping for a drink on the way to a wedding. He met their gaze so steadily that they turned back to the bar. At the far end he ordered a beer—the doctor had said no more whiskey—and sipped it until his eyes grew accustomed to the faint light. In the bar mirror he saw the grinning face of his driver,

16

who sat alone in a back booth. Boyle strolled over to him.

"Tony," he said.

"Went pretty good, didn't it?" Tony was a florid, beefy man with thick black hair. He wore a flowery Hawaiian shirt and white slacks over a bulging stomach, and gold rings gleamed on both hands.

"No, it didn't go pretty good," Boyle mimicked, sliding into the booth and glaring at the driver.

"Didn't it?" Tony held a pint of dark beer midway to his lips. "I thought it did, even with the breakdown."

"I hired you for driving."

"Sure you did. What's your gripe?"

"Tell me exactly what happened after you took over the bus in Reno."

"I didn't do nothing," Tony muttered. He gripped the beer schooner, his ringed fingers flashing. "I don't do nothing, but I get the blame."

"Start with Reno."

Tony nodded glumly and lit up a big cigar, which had the immediate effect of transforming him from a truck driver on vacation into the professional hood he actually was. He counted off the routes taken out of Reno around Lake Tahoe, northwest to Oroville, then southwest toward San Francisco. "Outside of Marysville I saw the sign for Knights Lodge and switched on the air conditioner like you said. I told them people earlier it was out of whack, but when I turned it on then nobody said nothing."

Boyle nodded. "People on a bus aren't very alert."

"I waited exactly one minute like you said. Then I put the mask on. It was dark, so I guess that's why they didn't see me do it. It fit right over my nose."

"They could have taken it for the bus mike."

"Sure, even if they seen it."

Boyle nodded with satisfaction, wondering how such a well-planned operation could go wrong.

"Maybe a minute later I heard these sounds, like when

17

you take in breath." Tony pursed his lips in the act of memory. "A couple whiffs of that gas and you're beddy-bye. You put that stuff on the market, you'd outsell any of them sleeping pills. I'd go for it. I got insomnia the pills won't touch."

"Go on, Tony."

He puffed gloomily on the cigar and described the rendezvous with the plumbing truck at the lake two miles beyond Knights Lodge. The three men in coveralls already had their gas masks on and carried medical bags. They climbed in the bus and started to check the passengers with stethoscopes. One old man wasn't breathing well, so they took a respirator from the truck and gave him oxygen. Then they rolled a large canvas hose into the bus, setting it midway along the aisle. Inside the truck an exhaust pump, attached to the hose, sucked the gas out of the bus in an hour. When it was cleared, Tony went into the bus with the plumbers and once again checked the passengers.

"They were okay?"

Tony nodded and motioned to the bartender for two more beers.

"Not for me," Boyle said.

"Don't tell me you're on the wagon. A lotta guys I know been going on the wagon. They think they're getting old, but the way I look at it, you're only as old as you feel."

"Go on, Tony."

He shrugged and blew a swirl of cigar smoke into the air, the pungent smell making Boyle regret that he had ever gone to a doctor who had forced him to give up not only cigarettes but his pipe as well. Tony began talking again. He described how the plumbers gave the gassed passengers hypodermic shots in their wrists. Then the plumbers rolled up the hose, shut the tailgate of the truck, and drove off.

"Real plumbers," Tony guffawed. "Then I sat down on a rock and waited. The moon came out. Bet there was some great fishing in that lake. I knew this Charlie Red from

18

Detroit, a great fisherman. Last I heard of him he was doing ten at Jackson."

"Go on, Tony."

"Like you told me to, I waited an hour for the stuff to work, then got in the bus and headed for Frisco."

"When did they start dying?"

"Right on schedule, about a half hour out of Frisco. I could see them through the mirror."

"Convulsions?"

"Ah, not much. A few fell outta the seats, but most just looked asleep."

"You checked them?"

"Like you said. Off the freeway on a side street. I took that thing the plumbers left me, that stet, stet—I can't say that fucking word—"

"Stethoscope."

"Yeah, and checked the hearts like you explained. Took maybe five minutes. Then I started out again and that's when the goddamn engine conked out. Lucky it did it there and not on the freeway. Then I called you and you came with the fuel hose and I put it in."

Boyle remembered that. Sitting in his car across the street, he had watched the faces begin to set like plaster while the street surfaced from the night.

"How'd you get the hose so damn fast, anyway?" Tony asked, sipping his new beer.

"A friend owes me."

Tony gave him a sly glance. "Yeah, I bet there's plenty owe you."

"Go on."

So he described the ensuing trip to the Coast Road and the rendezvous with the second truck. Two men had hauled the dead driver into the bus and set him behind the wheel; a minute later the truck had pushed the bus over the cliff. "Good thing they was fast," commented Tony, "because it was light already. Ten, fifteen minutes more we'd of

19

dumped those stiffs in the middle of traffic. We had luck on this one, but you gotta say it didn't go good."

"It did, except for the heist."

Tony shook his head sadly. "There you go. I didn't do nothing and you know it."

"Those tourists were found in the wreck robbed."

Tony arched his eyebrows and clicked his tongue. "I don't see how. Whattya think, I'd waste my time on *them* people, on chicken feed?"

That's what Boyle thought. Tony wouldn't risk his life unless the haul was worth it.

"Think I'd risk my reputation with you?" Tony said indignantly.

Boyle almost smiled: Tony's pride was that of a businessman whose credit has just been challenged.

"If you think I went for a few lousy wallets when I was almost pissing my pants worrying about cops, you got another think coming."

"All right, Tony. After fixing the hose, did you check the passengers again?"

"Sure. I know my business."

"And how did they look?"

"Dead."

"Their clothes, Tony."

"I don't know—slept in, I guess. But I found something in the aisle I was gonna give you. If you gave me half a chance," he added fretfully, then reached into his back pocket and came out with a small notebook. He threw it on the table. "I figured it was something one of them plumbers dropped and you'd want it back."

"Was there anything else?"

"Ah, some Kleenexes, maybe a pencil. The stuff people carry. I took the notebook figuring it might have names in it."

"Good."

"I know my business."

Boyle picked up the notebook and thumbed quickly through it. "You figured it belonged to a plumber. Why not a passenger?"

"It was in the aisle."

"But couldn't it fall out of someone's pocket?"

"They wasn't moving around much anymore. But the plumbers could of dropped it while they was working on the bus."

"You didn't see it in the aisle *before* you fixed the hose?"

Tony puffed on the cigar thoughtfully. "I get your meaning."

"What's that, Tony?"

"A punk could of got on the bus while I was phoning. He could of thrown stuff out of his own pockets to make room for what he took."

Boyle removed a wallet from his coat and handed a check to Tony.

"T. A. Willis," Tony read on the check and laughed. "I remember when you used the name S. R. Finley. Remember that time when we hit the guy in Monterey and you paid me on a Finley check?" Tony finished off his beer and leaned back, grinning expansively.

"Watch that," Boyle warned.

"Okay, okay, it just slipped out."

"Don't do it again," Boyle said coldly, rising. He didn't like the idea of Tony reminiscing like a retired salesman and he was angry at himself for wanting a smoke. On the way out he halted a moment and pulled a tobacco pouch from his back pocket. He grabbed a few toasted soybeans from the pouch and popped them into his mouth. Near the saloon door he turned for a last glimpse of the bulky man in the flowered shirt sitting over beer in a rear booth. Boyle knew this hood's way of life. Every night until the money ran out, that Hawaiian shirt would be draped over a chair in the infamous Mamma Wong's and Tony would be sitting naked on the bed, pawing a couple of handsome boys for a hundred dollars each.

During the cab ride back to the gallery, Boyle studied the frayed notebook. Aside from four phone numbers and the single name "Julie" written in large letters, the notebook was filled with crude drawings of animals and guns. Too amateurish for the hand of an artist, the drawings looked like the product of an obsessive mind. In page after page a lion or bear or giraffe was stalked by a machine gun, carbine, or pistol. There were no human figures.

When he got to the gallery, Boyle found his assistant in the office, feet propped up on the desk, whispering into the telephone. Boyle figured that Mr. Vertrees had a complicated sex life, full of intrigue and melodrama, which disabled him for serious work and relegated him to undemanding shopkeeping. Boyle often saw it on his face—the absorbing daydream of remembered humiliation, of imagined triumph. But Boyle was satisfied with him, because Mr. Vertrees knew his art, was personable, and above all possessed a youthful slimness that appealed to wealthy matrons. Boyle gave him the rest of the day off. Alone then in the office, Boyle opened the notebook to the phone numbers. The sudden craving for a smoke overwhelmed him. He knew that Mr. Vertrees kept a pack of cigarettes in the filing cabinet, but to smoke one of them would be a sacrilege, a damnation. He hadn't even smoked his pipe for nearly a year, but now this strict new diet was renewing his desire for an old vice.

"No," he said, and dialed the first number on the page. The information desk of the Fleishhacker Zoo answered, which startled him. He hesitated, then asked the girl what kind of information she could give him. She replied dryly that he could have the feeding schedules of the animals, the price of admission, opening and closing times, and any

22

office he desired. This confirmed the thief's obsessive interest in animals, but nothing more.

Alongside one of the phone numbers was a two-numeral extension, but he could decipher only the first digit because the second was smudged. He called, got the switchboard of a public library, and asked for extension three.

"Three what?" he was asked.

"How many extensions starting with three do you have?"

"Nine."

Boyle hung up and went to the filing cabinet, finding a half-opened pack of cigarettes immediately. He pulled one out, stared at it with dismay, then put it carefully between his lips. There was a folder of matches in the cabinet too, glowing like an open case of jewels. He snatched up the matches, swifty lit the cigarette, dragged until his eyes watered, then returned to the phone. The next number contacted him with the VA, but without an extension he didn't know whom to ask for, so he hung up. At least he knew that the thief was probably a veteran.

He dialed the last number, alongside the name Julie, and reached an answering service. The operator asked him to leave his own number and Miss Saunders would return the call. "Tell Miss Saunders it's urgent," Boyle said, then sat back and puffed gingerly on the cigarette that had already scoured his throat.

So the old familiar waiting had begun. Much of his life had been spent waiting for the sign that would galvanize him into action. Why couldn't he leave the past alone and enjoy the newfound peace of his later years? He was living again in the nightmare world of his youth and what now seemed unreal, a thing of the past, was this office with its paintings and sculpture.

The phone rang. He heard a girl's voice say rapidly in the crisp impatient tone of someone busy that she was Julie Saunders returning his call. "Who is this?" she asked.

"I'm an art dealer and I'd like to have your help."

"Mine? Who is this?"

"Alexander Boyle of the Boyle Gallery. I'm calling for some information."

"Who gave you my number?"

"That's what I'm calling about. Your name was in the notebook of a man I'm trying to locate."

There was a pause on the line, then the girl's voice, sharp with irritation. "Are you putting me on? I asked who gave you my number, that's all. Don't make a big deal of it."

"Look, this is rather complicated, but I mean what I say. Would it be asking too much if we meet and I explain?"

He heard the girl blow out her breath exasperatedly.

"If that's how you want to play it," she said. "Where?"

"Any place convenient for you. How about downtown?"

"Sure," she agreed lightly.

"I know a bar on California." He gave her the address, relieved that she wasn't being difficult. This was his only lead so far.

"Do they serve food? I'm starved."

"They do. In a half hour?"

"Why not?"

"How will I know you?"

"Oh, you'll know me, all right. I'm a great-looking blonde."

And she was, coming toward his booth in chino pants and a China-red blouse, when he waved to her. She carried a portfolio and a large canvas bag was slung from her shoulder. He guessed that Julie Saunders was a model, a guess she quickly confirmed. Sliding wearily into the booth and drawing a mirror out of her canvas bag, she began to describe her disheartening day as if they were old friends: a long wait for a botched interview, back to her stupid agent, then a cheap assignment with a sadistic photographer. "Anybody going into modeling ought to have her head examined. There's not much money in it, and you're out of a job most

24

of the time." Julie Saunders paused, looking up from her mirror and lipstick at last. "You're what I expected," she told Boyle with a smile.

"Oh?"

"I try to imagine people by their voices. Usually I'm disappointed, but not this time." She put aside the canvas bag and parted her moistened red lips. "You match your voice: the dark suit, the—strong face. Well," she waved her hand, "it all fits."

"And the thinning hair?"

"Sure. You sounded like a quiet, educated man in his mid-forties."

"A bit older, I'm afraid."

"See? I figured from your voice you'd put it all out front. The way some people try to disguise their age really gets me. Anyway, I like a little age in a man."

The waitress came over with menus.

Julie gave him a grimacing smile. "Fair warning. I'm hungry and I'm going to cost you."

Boyle ordered a beer for himself, and at her request a champagne cocktail. She chose the king-sized sirloin, "bloody inside, please," and all the trimmings, while Boyle took the Caesar salad.

"Ah, a weight-watcher," Julie crowed.

"No, I'm just not very hungry. Miss Saunders—"

"Julie."

"About that notebook—"

She cocked her head, as if puzzled. "Oh, yes, the notebook. I forgot the game you're playing."

"What?"

"Never mind. Say what you're going to say." She propped her head coyly in her hands and stared at him from cool blue eyes.

Boyle explained that last night while leaving his gallery two men had attacked him. They would have robbed and beaten him had not a passerby come to his aid. Together

25

they fought off the muggers; then the passerby left without a word and by the time Boyle recovered himself his defender was nowhere in sight. Boyle had, however, found a notebook the man had lost during the tussle and his purpose was to return it, along with heartfelt thanks.

The girl frowned. "But couldn't the notebook belong to one of the muggers?"

"I doubt if they'd have *your* number in it."

"Thank you, sir, for the vote of confidence." The drinks came and she drank half of hers in a single gulp. "I'm thirsty too," she said.

Boyle called the waitress to bring another champagne cocktail. Then he explained that he had learned only one thing from the notebook—the passerby was a veteran. "Do you know any veterans?"

Julie shrugged. "I suppose so. Some men say they are. I guess it's a status symbol. But when a man starts telling me about his war experience, I switch off. Nobody ever made an impression on me because he shot people."

"Ever know anyone interested in zoos?"

"Zoos?" Julie started to laugh, then stopped abruptly. "Hey, that's funny, but I do. A few weeks ago I went out to the Fleishhacker because I wasn't working and I was bored. I met a young guy there." She paused. "But he couldn't be the one you're looking for."

"Why not?"

"Well, you would have remembered him."

"It was dark, we were fighting. I don't remember a thing about him."

The girl's expression became wary. "Are you putting me on? Because you'd sure remember *him*. He wore this weird coat and a Jesus beard."

"Maybe he wasn't wearing the coat last night."

"I bet he was. He told me he wears it all the time. When I met him it was eighty degrees, but he had that coat on. He never told me why."

26

"Did you have a date with him?"

"I gave him my number, but he never called." The girl shrugged. "Anyway, I wouldn't have gone out with him."

"Why not?"

"Oh, he was kind of flaky. He was all wrapped up in tho animals. He said they ought to be let out. He said if anything should be in cages, it should be humans because they kill for pleasure and revenge instead of to live. Come to think of it, that's not so flaky. He really was a likable guy, but that coat!" She laughed merrily.

Boyle studied her, wondering if her story was true. She was a quick-witted girl who might have seen in his explanation of the notebook an attempt to locate the young man for quite another reason than the one he gave. She seemed to have liked the young man in spite of herself, and who knows, she might have seen him again, and now was protecting him.

"Did he say anything else?"

"Well, he wanted to see me again. For that matter, he wanted to see me that night. But he wasn't very persistent, he was kind of shy." Her eyes met Boyle's steadily. "I can't see him walking into a fight."

Boyle ignored that, asking if the young man had told her anything else; had he, for example, told her where he lived?

"Yes, he mentioned something about that." She paused thoughtfully. "He said he had a room in some hotel in North Beach. I think he was hinting," she added with a wink.

The food came, and Boyle watched enviously as she plowed into that richly marbled steak, french fries, and creamed peas. He let her draw him into a discussion of art, figuring that she might be testing his knowledge of it in an attempt to authenticate his story about the art gallery, the attacks, and the passerby. But then again she might just be making conversation. In this kind of work it was easy to become paranoid. Watching her eat, Boyle found himself con-

27

centrating on her beauty and gusto and freshness. Since his wife had died, he had rarely gone out with a woman. In the last few years he could count on two hands the number of times he had made love. From the moment she had appeared in the bar, Julie Saunders had appealed to him, possibly because she seemed to be attracted to him, too. Was that possible? A girl that age?

After she had finished off the steak, Boyle ordered strawberry shortcake for her. How wonderful it was to be young, to eat anything! He pulled out a cigarette and lit it, watching the strawberries disappear. When she finished, Julie Saunders gave him a sudden look of appraisal. She seemed to be struggling toward a decision.

"What's on your mind?" Boyle asked abruptly.

The girl frowned. "You."

"What about me?"

"Listen, I don't know why, but I want to be out front with you."

Here it comes, Boyle thought.

"I wish you would be," he said.

"Really? Maybe I'm making a fool of myself, but I don't care. I like you. I like you very much. I want you to know the truth. When you called, I thought you were looking for someone."

"Well, I was."

"No, I don't mean looking for that kid. I thought you were looking for a *girl,* and you knew from someone I was available." She bit her lip and looked away from him at the bar, the tables, the bustling crowd. "This is a real nice place."

The truth was dawning on him: Julie Saunders had readily agreed to meet him because she was a call girl.

Her eyes swung back to meet his steadily. "Does it shock you?"

"No, but I'm surprised. There's a difference."

"Thank you for that. I just wanted you to know. You see," her voice was muted, hesitant, "I like you."

"I'm glad you do." Boyle reached over to take her hand, but she pulled it away.

"Don't be condescending."

"I'm not, I'm really glad."

After studying him a moment, she nodded. "Sorry. I guess I'm suspicious of kindness. It has to do with the men I meet. Sooner or later they stop being kind and get moral. They'll jump into bed and pay me for it, then all of a sudden they want to know why I do it. And when I ask them is there a quicker way for a poor girl to earn enough money for some world traveling, they look at me like I just robbed a bank."

Boyle said nothing.

"Well, are you judging me, too?"

He shook his head and this time she let him take her hand. He wished he could match her honesty. He'd like to reassure her that what she was doing was no more than misguidedly practical compared to what he had seen of the world, its brutalities and betrayals.

"What are you thinking?" she asked suddenly.

He wanted to tell her she was lovely, because a single remark of that sort might very well set romance in motion. He knew that *in minutes* this girl could make the years recede and recapture for him those feelings he had had when courting Cora with his whole heart. And that would leave him even a bigger fool than he'd been the other morning when he failed to check the bus. So he didn't answer her question, but merely sat there solemnly uncommunicative while slowly she withdrew her hand from his. "Well, sorry to eat and run," Julie said airily and gathered up her bag and portfolio. For a moment her eyes met his, and when he still said nothing, she got up from the booth. "Thanks for the steak," she told him crisply. "I was starved."

"Julie, what was his name?"

She put one hand on her hip, exasperatedly. "I can't figure you out."

"I really do want to thank him," Boyle persisted.

"Well—" Her eyes stared into the distance. "His name was—let me think—Warren. It was Warren."

"And his last name?"

"For godssakes, how should I know?" she replied irritably.

Boyle smiled up at her, feeling the blood in his cheeks. "Julie, maybe we'll meet again."

"I doubt it. Pardon me, will you, for being a fool?"

Grimly controlled, Boyle watched her lithe figure move toward the entrance. She did not glance back. Had she told him the truth about the kid? He waited until she was gone before calling for the check. "Bring me a pack of cigarettes. Any brand." Then taking out a dime, he went to the phone booth.

"Hirschorn? Boyle again. I've had a break. Could you help me find a North Beach hotel?"

"Alex, the fewer people in this, the better. I could help but I'd have to get an okay first. Think you can do it on your own?"

"Sure," Boyle agreed, aware that the whole affair could blow sky-high.

"You say you've had a break?" said Hirschorn.

"I think the thief is a young war veteran."

"Well, that sounds like progress. What about your driver?"

"What about him?" Boyle said.

"Don't get touchy. I'm just asking if you're going to make *complete* payment tonight, like you said?"

"When I say I will, I will."

"He's not mixed up with this war veteran, is he?"

"He's clean."

After a long pause Hirschorn said, "I know how you feel about it."

"Sure," said Boyle, convinced, however, that no one could know how it felt to be in such a position. Not that he couldn't justify what was going to happen to Tony Aiello, a cheap hood whose death wouldn't be worth a line on the back page. But over the years Boyle had seen him change from a thin, determined, controlled professional, whose unquestioning obedience you could count on, into a garrulous, overweight, red-faced hustler, who liked to sit in a bar and reminisce like a failed salesman. When you see tendencies become full-blown unhealthy traits and flighty mannerisms replace solid hallmarks of character, you feel for a man— that's how he felt about Tony, however grudgingly. He imagined Tony lounging on a rumpled bed in Mamma Wong's, pawing a rouged boy, innocently happy.

"I'm damn sorry I took this job," Boyle chafed. "Right from the start I knew better."

"Yes, but you took it," Hirschorn pointed out with blunt simplicity. "Look at your driver another way. He might spill the beans accidentally. We couldn't take that risk. Even if there wasn't one helluva lot better reason, that would be reason enough."

It was true, of course. Boyle again imagined Tony lying back, with one fat hand caressing a girlish thigh, while he bragged of driving a mysterious bus full of pretty weird passengers. It helped Boyle to think that the job was too important to entrust to Tony's discretion. Tony had aged into unreliability.

"One thing more about your driver," said Hirschorn. "Be sure you do it the way Spitz suggested."

"Hell, yes. There wouldn't be much point otherwise."

"Don't get sore, Alex. Good luck. When this mess about the property is straightened out, I'm buying the drinks."

"Beer for me."

"Say, that's right. You're living the clean life."

Boyle had another break, finding the North Beach hotel on his third try. Earlier in the century it had been a sailor's home, but now it was a flophouse for drifters. When Boyle walked into the squalid lobby, the clerk eyed him warily. At the flash of Boyle's fake police badge, the clerk sneered.

"I'm looking," said Boyle, "for a kid in a beard and a long coat. You got him here?"

The clerk shrugged. "Not that I know of." He was a lean man sunken back into a suit that matched the gray of his wrinkled skin. Boyle knew the type. They liked to withhold information just for the hell of it. Some of them got more pleasure from being uncooperative than they did from getting paid for what they knew. But this one looked hungry. Boyle threw a twenty on the desk. "The kid's first name is Warren."

The clerk snatched up the money. "Warren," he said. "Why didn't you say so? Sure, he's been here about a month." He opened the register and turned pages. "There. Warren Shore. Got a beard. Always nursing a cold."

"A cold?"

"Not what you think. We don't let them drug freaks in here. This kid got a *regular* cold. He concentrates on it. He comes through the lobby here blowing his—"

"Is he in?"

The clerk shook his head.

"When did he go out?"

"About noon."

"Got any idea when he might come back?"

"How many questions do I gotta answer?"

Boyle threw a ten on the desk.

"He checked out."

"At noon?"

"That's right. He come down here and checked out and got in a nice new Chevy."

"New? He had a new car?"

"He didn't have no car till today."

"When he left, did he have that coat on?"

"I never seen him when he didn't."

"Forwarding address?"

The clerk chuckled. "Sure, the Ritz."

A young man slouching in blue jeans, his hair below his

32

shoulders, came through the front door and leaned on the desk wearily. He could hardly stand up, as he mumbled thickly for his key. The clerk gave him the key and he shuffled away, head down, hands dangling. Boyle and the clerk watched him mount the stairs slowly, like an old woman.

"Kids today ain't got style anymore," said the clerk. "Look at 'em. They're all a bunch of pigs. They piss in the halls, throw food all over." He shook his head righteously. "They make me sick."

"Can you tell me any more about Warren Shore?"

"What's to tell? Like I say, he goes around nursing that cold. From what I saw of him, he never did nothing else."

Again Boyle had a break. He found the car rental agency a few blocks from the hotel. The agent on duty was a pink-cheeked young man whose response to Boyle's badge was immediate and fervent. "How can I help, sir?" He spread his hands out proprietarily on the counter, his lips compressed. He quickly found the contract for Warren Shore's rental. Boyle noted down the registration and engine number.

"We have his stated destination," the rental agent said. "In the North Beach area we try to find out what they'll do with the cars. Naturally a lot of them lie but you'd be surprised how many of them run off with a car and we track them to the city they say they're heading for."

"Which in this case is—?"

"San Diego."

Boyle had been lucky. He knew something now about the thief's appearance, habits, and destination—enough to be able to find him. If everything went as smoothly tomorrow and possibly the next day, Boyle would have those stolen goods back and everyone could forget the whole affair. He had been so proud of the job, worked out on such short notice; but an ordinary fuel line hose had brought him this extra worry. That's how it was sometimes; you had a

33

good plan and then a tiny detail loomed out of nowhere and made havoc of it.

He caught a bus out to the Portola district where he had a floor-through apartment in a small three-story house owned by an Italian family that kept a superb wine cellar and invited him to dinner once a month. It was dark by the time he got home and in the street light his landlady's two sons were shooting baskets through a hoop over the garage. He waved to them, then entered the house and climbed a flight to his apartment. He walked in, turned on a lamp in the living room, and flung himself down on the couch. He was tired and hungry; that Caesar salad he'd eaten with Julie Saunders, while she polished off a pound and a half of sirloin, hadn't satisfied him. But all he kept in the apartment, purposely, was vegetarian soup. He pulled off his shoes and propped up his feet on the coffee table. In the old days Cora would sit beside him on the couch and gently knead the pain out of his muscles. He glanced at her photo on the desk below a print by a Mexican artist. Cora looked back at him, her dark eyes luminous, her lips parted in a skeptical smile.

Boyle opened the new pack of cigarettes and lit up. Not in a year had the smell of smoke drifted through *this* apartment. He rose and went into the kitchen, fumbled through the bottom cabinet for the Scotch hidden behind the safflower oil. He kept the Scotch for artists and clients who dropped in for a drink. But what the hell, he deserved a drink in view of the nasty job facing him in a few hours. He measured out exactly one ounce in a glass, splashed a little water over it, and returned to the living room. He picked up the phone and called Mr. Vertrees.

The phone rang and rang, but Boyle knew enough to hang on. Finally Vertrees answered, his voice low, breathless, expectant, somewhat coquettish. But when he heard Boyle, his voice steadied. Boyle explained that business would take him out of town a few days. Boyle discussed a few

34

problems, a client to be called, a woodcut to be framed, a brochure to be proofread. "I don't know how long I'll be gone," Boyle said. "No, I'll have to call you. I'm not sure where I'm staying. Don't forget to save the review of the Diebenkorn show, if I'm not back for it. Call Kawabata and put some pressure on him. If he hasn't got ten paintings done by the end of the month, I'm canceling him out. Yes. Tell him that. There's only one way to deal with that alcoholic Jap, and that's to scare him."

After the call, Boyle went back to the kitchen, searched behind the safflower oil again, and made himself another drink, this time without measuring. He needed something to calm himself down, because he was nervous as a cat, anticipating the rest of the evening. He went into the bedroom, lay down on the bed, set the alarm clock for midnight, and sipped his drink until falling asleep.

When the alarm went off, he jumped out of bed and in the bathroom doused his face with cold water. Then he made some Sanka and drank it laced with skim milk. There was no need to hurry, but he felt restless, light-headed, as if he were going into combat. After twenty-five years he could still remember how it was before a patrol began. From the bottom drawer of a dresser he took out his .450 Webley Scott with the 2-1/4-inch barrel, his favorite weapon for years. Bullets from a gun of high muzzle-velocity penetrated too cleanly, in his opinion, and left only small perforations in tissue as they traveled through, whereas bullets from his W & S didn't waste their effect on scenery beyond the target, but tore gaping holes on impact. It wasn't a flashy or handsome gun; it just went about its business like an old professional. He screwed a silencer on it and jammed it into a belt holster. From another drawer he got a pair of rubber gloves, then hauled a five-gallon can of kerosene out of the silent house and set it on the front seat of the Plymouth which he had rented that afternoon under the name of S. R.

Finley. His own car was parked in a Bayshore garage miles away.

Then he drove down into the waterfront area and parked under the skyway, hearing overhead the steady rumble of cars. It was after one o'clock. Through the open car window drifted the waterfront air, redolent of spices, of ginger and coffee stacked in warehouses. He wanted a smoke, but suppressed that goddamned urge, and rested his head on the seat top, like someone preparing to nap. But he kept an eye on the entrance of an old clapboard building wedged between warehouses across the street. Time passed, the air took on a chill, so he rolled up the window. The thud of wheels overhead became intermittent, then discontinuous for intervals as long as half a minute. A squall blew up from the bay, and for a half hour the rain beat against the windshield, then the air was still. Through the glistening window glass he finally saw a man emerge from the clapboard building.

In the entranceway of Mamma Wong's the man paused to light a cigarette. The half-moon flare of the match illuminated Tony Aiello's heavy face. He was smiling. Then he turned down the dark street, his slow footsteps clicking hollowly in the valley between the ranked black warehouses. He was whistling. Without turning the headlights on, Boyle started the car and headed for him. When alongside, he called Tony's name and jumped out of the car. Tony hesitated, slipped his hand inside his coat, but upon seeing a familiar face in the dim light, withdrew his hand. "Oh, it's you," he said with a breath of relief.

In one motion Alexander Boyle, the Sanitation Man, had the Webley & Scott out in front of his chest, left hand cradling the right which held the gun. Because of the poor light he decided first on a gut shot, and it blew Tony off the sidewalk, back against a brick wall. The Sanitation Man stood over the slumped body, and this time took deliberate aim, arcing the muzzle from a spot slightly above the head

36

down to the center of the face. With the sound of a door slamming, he put one more bullet into Tony, ripping the face out and leaving a large ragged hole where a smile of contentment had so recently been.

Quickly he dragged the body over to the car, stuffed it into the backseat, and got back into the still idling car. He drove away fast. There was no traffic on the freeway, so he reached the railroad yards in Bayshore within minutes. On a street lined with warehouses, vacant lots, and closed lunchrooms he parked in view of the switchyards, the freight cars gloomily visible like stolid buffalo on a dark plain. He sat a minute, looking in the rearview mirror at the huddled body behind him. Then he unscrewed the cap of the five-gallon can and by leaning its weight on the top of the seat, poured kerosene over Tony Aiello. When the liquid had soaked thoroughly into the clothes, he poured some of it over the upholstery. He repeated the process, then emptied what was left on the front seat. He threw the rubber gloves, worn ever since leaving his apartment house, inside the car after getting out of it. From his pocket he took a piece of paper, shaped it into a wick, lit it, and tossed it through the open window. The flame whooshed up with the sound of a brush fire, and as he looked back from the corner he was turning at a trot, the intense conflagration reminded him of photographs of Buddhists immolating themselves. So that was the end of Tony Aiello—Tony, who had never wanted much more than a few boys in a back room of Mamma Wong's and a solid reputation among people who could use his talents.

That was what Boyle was still thinking of—Tony's shabby but oddly fulfilled life—when he arrived fifteen minutes later at the garage where his own car had been parked since late afternoon. Waiting for the sleepy attendant to get the car, Boyle studied himself in the garage light. He had come out of it clean, not a drop of blood on him, except for a single dark stain the size of a quarter on his left sleeve. It

37

was daybreak by the time he reached home, but before going to bed he took a hot shower and removed the sleeve stain with cleaning fluid. Ever since boyhood he had been meticulous in his appearance and personal hygiene. One of his worst memories was of the mud in Normandy during World War II, the mud and the smell of his own body and an especially vivid recollection of blood from a wound soaking through his uniform, drying there like something he had spilled while eating.

Light was glowing on the drawn shades as he flung himself wearily on the bed. Again he thought of Tony, convinced finally that since he'd had to choose someone to be the doomed driver, he had made the right choice. Tony Aiello was a man who had lost his style. Secure in this knowledge, Boyle fell into a dreamless sleep.

3

Warren stood on the strip of white beach called the Silver Strand, which connects the town of Coronado to the suburbs south of San Diego. It was hardly dawn, but he had dragged himself out of bed in order to see the sunrise and to watch for whales. Lowering above him, however, was a cloud-filled sky, and the surface of the Pacific had been whitened by a thick fog to the dun color of dust. Slow but heavy waves were coming in, their curls breaking sluggishly, sending out lazy streamers of surf. He pulled the lapels of his coat close against the chill morning air and searched the gray horizon for whales. He had read somewhere that you can watch them migrating along the Southern California coast, bound for Mexican waters to breed. This was the right season. He strained to catch a heart-lifting glimpse of their immense gunmetal sides, but the fog kept rolling in, enveloping the coast like a giant amoeba. Warren squatted on the sand, glancing back now and then at the grass being blown against the dunes by a gust of morning wind. Not far from him he saw a large gull flat-footed on the beach, facing the ocean as if it too were waiting for a sight of whales. The gull's white breast swelled aggressively, its yellow beak curved like a sickle, its forehead sloped malignantly. Its head turned suddenly and fixed Warren with an angry red eye. Warren glared back in challenge, but the bird never moved. Warren got to his feet, but the bird never moved. Warren hissed, but the bird merely rotated its head slightly and looked again at the ocean.

In Vietnam Warren had often dreamed of birds. One dream reoccurred. He lay on a bare floor in an empty room and around him flew countless birds of every variety, all fluttering and squawking, slamming in their wild flight against the walls. He wanted to get up and run from the room, but he couldn't move, not even when some of the birds, small and sparrow-quick, alighted on his chest, and not even when they hopped on his face, bobbing down to peck at his eyes. At this point in the dream he always awakened, heart hammering violently. Birds were the only animals he didn't admire. In their chatter and mechanical movement and cold expression, they reminded him of humans.

He picked up a piece of driftwood, slinging it hard at the gull. It didn't move. Warren threw another piece, this time barely missing the gull, who at last took wing and flapped off in the direction of the Del Coronado Hotel, rising purple-spired above the sand dunes to the north. That damn hotel, Warren thought. Last night he tried to get a room there, but they wouldn't take him, not even when he guaranteed he had the money. So he had gone to a broken-down motel in Imperial Beach. When he called his aunt last night (she had made him promise), Warren couldn't restrain himself, but burst into an angry diatribe against Americans, who worshipped money and judged by appearances. He told her that taking the money and goods from those bus passengers was the first intelligent thing he had done since leaving the hospital. He had shouted down her protest. Poor Aunt Victoria, she had never known any peace with him, not while he had been growing up and certainly not now, when he was armed against her naive morality by his bitterly earned knowledge of the world.

Suddenly he felt tired. He had never regained his energy after leaving the hospital. His body played tricks on him. One moment he would feel fine and the next moment, without warning, his legs nearly buckled, his head throbbed, and his cold grew worse. After one last, disappointed glance at the gray ocean, he trudged over the dunes to his car and returned to the motel for a nap. Rolling onto the bed, he wished once again that the blonde had come with him. He imagined her beside him. Lying there together it wouldn't matter if she was taller than he. Had she been with him on the beach, her hair alive in the morning wind, he wouldn't have felt tired. And now, stretched out on the bed, in the silence, he could have moved over slightly and touched her warm side. He could have told her that even though the world was cruel, there was a place in it for love. And then he could have taken her in his arms.

When he awoke, the sun had burned away the fog and the sky was spotlessly blue.

Alexander Boyle got to the San Diego Zoo at noon, hoping that he wasn't too late. At the entrance he paused to study the best place to station himself. To the right was a restaurant and to the left a souvenir shop where he bought sunglasses and a visored cap, blending him into the crowd which began to pour through the gateway, bearing their cameras and other paraphernalia like so many nomads shuffling into a migration. Boyle hesitated near the information booth, looking beyond it to the tree-shrouded canyons and mesas of the zoo. The balmy air was scented by tropical flowers and filled with the cries of monkeys. He moved over in front of the camera shop where he rented a pair of binoculars. Slowly he walked to and fro, keeping on the move but never losing sight of the inpouring crowd. Now and then from the corner of his eye he caught a glimpse of the flamingos shimmering in their lagoon. An hour passed, but the right beard never came through the gate. He saw clipped beards and goatees and pointed Spanish cuts, but no wild "Jesus beard," as Julie Saunders had described. Finally he saw one, but the young man was tall and wore an open sports shirt without a coat. The unending stream of visitors began to look all alike to him. It wasn't easy to concentrate on so many faces surrounded by all that noise and color. The day was growing hot, he was thirsty and hungry, and he began to turn frequently for a quick glance at a hot dog stand, where a crowd of crying kids and bored fathers and distraught mothers were milling around, holding balloons and stuffed animals, reaching out for mustard-smeared franks and cold bottles of Coke.

By two o'clock Boyle was nervous, if not yet discouraged. Perhaps Shore had come earlier in the day or would only come tomorrow or just possibly never come at all. Boyle had been confident of his hunch. On the evidence of those obsessive drawings in the notebook and after his talk with Julie Saunders, Boyle would have made book that the kid would head straight for the greatest zoo in the world if he was anywhere near San Diego. Could he have gone elsewhere? But why would he have lied to the auto agent? He couldn't know he was being followed.

Boyle was turning these thoughts over as he ambled toward the hot dog stand. Then suddenly he was there, confronting the smell of sizzling frankfurters, rubbing elbows with people carrying away hot food and cold drinks. A single frank wouldn't make his cholesterol soar, though it was laden with saturated fat. He had to keep his strength up for a job like this. With one eye still on the entrance, Boyle plunked down money for one frank and a Coke. The bun felt warm in his hand. He took a swig of ice-cold Coke, then bit into the frankfurter, tasting the pungent yellow mustard just as his gaze fixed upon the young man, short and black-bearded, wearing a trench coat that reached to his ankles, moving swiftly through the incoming crowd.

He turned right at the entrance plaza, walked past the restaurant, and headed for Mesa E with hardly a glance at the penguins and kiwis. He had arrived late, so he couldn't expect to see much of the zoo today. He could, of course, take the bus tour, but that was no way to see a zoo, not this zoo certainly, and anyway there was always tomorrow and the day after that and the day after that until he knew by heart where everything was, until he had savored the sights and sounds and smells and movement of this entire world. He was too excited by the prospect to see much at first. He rushed along the paths, absorbing the color and grandeur, walked beneath towering trees, past enclosures full of the scrub and grass of an African veld, through the tangled foliage of a tropical rain forest. He quick-timed along paths bordered by frangipani trees and beds of exotic wax flowers, and ascended by moving stairways to mesas from which he had glimpses of exhibits in wooded canyons below.

Suddenly he felt tired; a wave of fatigue so swept him that he had to stop and rest awhile on a bench. Sitting there he contemptuously studied the passing crowd, all jabbering more witlessly than monkeys. These people moved like robots, and aside from some of the children, they displayed little curiosity; it was a stroll in the air for them, a smell of sugary mimosa, a cry of recognition at the sight of a commonly known animal. None of them shared his own sense of beauty, his admiration, even his longing to be so free of cant and malicious cruelty. And yet they all must laugh at his beard and coat, snicker behind his back as they pulled the strings of their balloons and stuffed their faces with gouts of hamburger. Well, let them; he didn't care. That man with the sunglasses had been looking at him, he was certain. People often stole a look at him, unaware that his own eyes were sharp, trained to catch detail, even the

43

rustle of a leaf, to notice the shape of death, like the outline of a metal disk buried just under the surface of a rice paddy. Let them go ahead and sneak looks at him. He didn't care. But sometimes he wondered if they thought something peculiar was under his coat. Now and then he had the queer sensation of being naked under it, and curious eyes could catch a glimpse of the zigzag welt, of the disgusting ugliness.

Warren watched disdainfully as the man in sunglasses and visored cap strolled by, a pair of binoculars dangling from his neck, his expensive dark suit incongruous for a zoo and in a way impertinent. I ought to get up, Warren thought, and ask that man why he came to the zoo. "Did you come to see the animals, mister? Well, look around you. Those are the *real* animals, the ones walking beside you."

The imagined scene gave Warren new energy, so he rose from the bench and continued his tour, this time heading for Canyon K, where the big cats were. He descended into a majestic stand of eucalypti and for a long time lingered in front of the heavily furred Siberian tigers and sinuous Chinese leopards. The enclosures simulated natural habitats and no more than moats separated them from the public, a situation that denied Warren his fantasy of freeing the cats from their barred cages. But that was all right with him. It was quite enough to watch them blinking their yellow eyes, displaying their white fangs when they yawned. He was certain that they dreamed of a more beautiful world than their viewers could ever imagine. Warren felt tired again. That doctor in the army hospital who had told him fatigue was often psychosomatic was a damn liar. His body was a complete wreck, but the army didn't want to admit it. He had seen the doctors joking with paraplegics, as if paralysis from the waist down was no more than a bad cold. He would never forget one of the doctors saying to a paraplegic, who refused to move his wheelchair, "Come on, corporal, it's a piece of cake."

Warren took out a Kleenex, blew so furiously that his ears popped. His damn cold was acting up again. The only thing that helped when it got this bad was a drink, so Warren headed for the main gate. In the entrance plaza he paused at the souvenir shop to turn the pages of a zoo brochure. With that special sense developed on jungle patrol, Warren knew someone was watching him. But he kept turning pages awhile, and when at last he walked away, he swung around suddenly, catching a glimpse of the man in sunglasses and visored cap. He was sure the man had been staring at him, although when Warren turned, the man seemed to be buying something at the hot dog stand. Well, let him stare, Warren thought, let them all stare. Although he loved the zoo, Warren was relieved to get out of it at this moment. If only he could be here when everyone else had gone. It would be a great thing to walk the empty paths in darkness and hear on every side the shrill cries of the jungle.

For nearly six hours Boyle had sat in his car across the street from the tavern. One of its dirty windows was filled with a red neon sign advertising a beer and the other gave him a view of Warren Shore's back, hunched over the bar. Now and then the kid turned his head, as if talking to someone, and raised a beer mug, as if toasting. Boyle couldn't tell if the kid was eating while he drank. Boyle felt justified in having taken two frankfurters with him as he had followed Shore out of the zoo into the parking lot. On a job like this it was *impossible* to follow a diet. From across the street he heard the blare of rock music, a youthful noise that didn't appeal to him. Probably it appealed to Shore, but then again it might not. The kid was strange; swallowed up in a coat more appropriate to Maine than California, he had stood in front of the animals as if communing with them. But he was alert, possibly cunning. Had he turned at the main gate so suddenly for a reason? Had he seen me? Boyle wondered. Did I tail him too closely? Did I make a mistake by wearing the sunglasses and cap?

Probably there was nothing to worry about; if the kid had been suspicious, surely he would have tried to shake the tail instead of ambling into the first tavern he saw. Boyle sat up. There he was at last, the coat buttoned up and flapping at his ankles. In the street light Boyle saw that the kid was scowling through the black beard. He walked as if he wanted to get away from the tavern fast. Had he been in an argument? Although Julie Saunders had contended that the kid wasn't the belligerent sort, Boyle figured him for a short fuse. At least he was twitchy enough to wear on the nerves of people who were drinking. The kid had trouble unlocking his car. After getting in, he slammed the door angrily and drove off at a wild, weaving clip. Boyle followed, hoping the cops wouldn't stop the kid. They'd book him for drunken driving, a complication Boyle didn't want to face. But luckily Shore navigated through the city without incident, got himself across the arcing Coronado Bridge, and pulled up safely in front of the Del Coronado Hotel.

Boyle watched the flapping coat disappear into the majestic building, then followed. He found the kid bent over the bar in the Casino lounge. Quickly Boyle slipped into a chair at a table in shadows near the entrance. No more than a dozen people were sitting in the high-beamed cosy room under a golden light. Their voices hummed with a timeless summer elegance. A waiter in red vest came for Boyle's order. After a moment's hesitation, he ordered a Scotch on the rocks, then sat back to watch Shore, who sat hunched up midway along the bar, empty stools on either side of him. The Scotch came and Boyle had looked down at it, his hand reaching for the thick, iced glass, when suddenly the genteel atmosphere was shattered by a shrill, querulous voice. "Did you hear me? I ordered a drink here!"

The white-coated bartender, who had been hovering at the far end of the bar, shuffled toward the kid, whose sulky profile was facing Boyle. The bartender leaned toward Shore and whispered something. Immediately the young man tossed money on the bar. "Does *that* satisfy you?" he snapped, and heads around the room turned again. The bartender hesitated, then started to make a drink. Shore swiveled on the stool and glared defiantly. For a moment Boyle thought that the kid was studying him, but then the bartender set a drink on the bar and Shore scooped it up, jerked his head back, and drank it down with a gulp. Then he emitted a long, growling belch that resonated obscenely through the room. He followed this with a high nervous giggle, which brought the bartender back to him swiftly. This time Boyle could hear, "You will have to leave, sir!"

"I want another."

"Sir, please don't make trouble for yourself." Boyle saw the bartender's hand disappear under the bar, probably searching for a buzzer.

For a moment Shore remained motionless, then he swung off the stool and with a thunderous "To hell with it," started for the entrance of the lounge.

Boyle looked down at his drink, sensing, however, that the kid had halted a few feet away.

"Haven't I seen you before?"

Boyle slowly looked up, meeting Shore's eyes that gleamed faintly in the golden light. "Are you talking to me?" he said calmly.

"I've seen *you* before," Shore declared, pointing at him with his forefinger.

Boyle shrugged and studied his drink again.

Shore moved closer, his face twisting in concentration. "I saw you at the zoo today."

"The zoo?" Boyle grinned, then waved away the ap-

47

proaching waiter. The last thing he wanted now was a scene. "What zoo?"

"I remember that suit. I remember your face, only you were wearing sunglasses and a dumb hat."

"I'm sorry, but I never saw you before in my life."

"You had binoculars."

Boyle met his eyes steadily but didn't reply.

"Oh, to hell with it!" With a parting glower, Shore headed out of the lounge.

Boyle took a quick sip of his drink, deciding what to do. If he started after the kid, there might be a scene, but if he let the kid get a start on him, he might lose the trail. So he had to risk it. Tossing a five on the table, Boyle rose and went into the lobby, catching a glimpse of Shore's swaying figure disappearing through the main entrance. Boyle gave him a minute, then followed, emerging into the night where he expected to see Shore's car driving away.

But it was still there.

Where had the kid gone? Boyle turned right, circling the hotel toward the ocean side. Ahead was the Beach and Tennis Club; its spire lit it up brilliantly. Boyle started to trot, seeing a flapping figure to the right of the building. When he got to the edge of the club, he could see the kid, head down, striding past the Turquoise Pool and cabanas toward the ocean. Boyle halted in the shadows of the cabanas, allowing Shore to proceed alone down the long stretch of beach to the water. Boyle waited while the kid squatted at the ocean's edge and stared out toward the moonlit horizon. I could take him now, Boyle thought, but then I wouldn't find the goods.

"Who do they think they are?" Warren said out loud, throwing a pebble viciously at the water. In the tavern someone had laughed at him for defending the Boy Scouts. Well, why shouldn't he? Only thing he had ever really done in life was become an Eagle. It wasn't easy to become

48

an Eagle. Nobody believed in anything anymore or an Eagle Scout would still be respected. Aunt respected him for being an Eagle. She had been proud of every merit badge he had earned, and when he stood before the District Director to have his medal pinned on, Aunt had cried.

The dirty bastards laughing at him in the tavern had looked like pigs at a trough, swilling their goddamn beer. They didn't know how animal-like they looked. One of them had the long pointed ears and slant eyes of a jackal. Another had the yellowish head and curved cruel mouth of a tortoise. Another the heavy jaws and slick puffy skin of a hippo. He knew them all for what they were: counterfeits of the true, the honest animals. And then that bunch in the Del Coronado, soft as seals, mean as African hunting dogs. And he had seen that man from the zoo again, hadn't he? Without sunglasses the man looked like an owl, with those large cold eyes and small tight mouth. What was he, a queer trying to pick someone up?

To hell with them all. He was glad now that Julie hadn't come with him, because she'd be as phony as the rest. Looking out at the ocean, shimmering like snow under the moon, he tried to imagine Julie, only the image in his mind was of a cheetah, lithe and frail-looking, suddenly lunging into a deadly run. Warren rose to his feet, throwing one more pebble at the immense expanse of water. Then he walked back to the hotel and drove the car along the strand into Imperial Beach. He was glad now he hadn't wasted his money on the Del Coronado; the little motel was better, more honest, like the animals in the zoo who were dreaming of jungles. Inside his room Warren flung off the coat and picked up the phone. He put in a call to San Francisco.

"Aunt? Warren. How are you? Sure I'm all right. I just thought I'd call. No, I'm *not* lonely. What the hell, I went to the zoo today. What? It was great. Fantastic. I may stay around here a long time." Warren giggled. "I found a home in the San Diego Zoo. Oh, come on, Aunt, I just had a few beers. Don't you want me to socialize? I met some beautiful people here. I—no, I'm not being sarcastic. I've made a conquest. What? I said, *conquest*. A guy at the zoo has been following me. Sure. No, I'm not kidding. I know, I know, but there's nothing to worry about. I just stopped and faced him with it. Sure I'm sure he was trying to pick me up. No, nothing to do with *that*. Don't you worry about me. Sure, I will. I'll call tomorrow. Yes, I know. I'll be careful. Good-bye."

Warren was glad he had called her, even though she fussed over him too much and worried about nothing. People like his aunt were few and far between. They were too good for the human world—they belonged in the zoo. He laughed out loud in surprise and delight at the good sense of the idea, while pulling off his shirt and trousers. In the bathroom he rinsed his mouth out, then glanced shyly at his naked body. "To hell with it," he muttered and shuffled from the bathroom, flinging himself down on the bed. A full day on patrol couldn't have exhausted him more. What ailed him was obviously his body and not his mind, let the army doctors say what they pleased. What did they know, puffing on pipes behind desks in air-conditioned rooms? They should go out in the rice paddies awhile until the weather of that country swam in their own blood before telling someone how nervous he was. Maybe he had contracted a weird tropical disease, which would explain the terrible colds and sudden bouts of fatigue.

Moonlight fell across his body, when he turned off the bedside lamp. He looked down at a dark jagged slash from groin to ribs and suddenly thought of Julie. What would she say about it if she were with him now? Probably she wouldn't say a thing, but his scar would secretly disgust her. That's how people always reacted to imperfections. In this world you are judged by appearance, not by what you really are.

Warren sniffed tentatively, then breathed in deeply through his nose. It surprised him, the ease of his breathing. His nostrils were so clear tonight he wouldn't need Privine. He might even sleep well, although too much drinking often gave him nightmares. From what he had seen of people today, he might dream of their ugliness—or of birds. Or maybe with luck he would dream of Julie approaching through the moonlight and his unscarred healthy body would meet hers with the delicious abandon of two dogs in the street. He smiled, closed his eyes, and almost instantly fell asleep.

Warren was dreaming of birds when the door opened.

The Sanitation Man's second shot at close range had shattered the heart, flinging blood everywhere. In the bathroom, with gloves still on, he discovered a number of spots on his coat. Dabbing them with a wet washrag, he satisfied himself that he was sufficiently clean to continue the job. Returning to the other room, he turned on the light and looked down at the kid, naked, sprawled halfway between the bed and the door. His agility had surprised Boyle, but on second thought it was reasonable that a man accustomed to combat would retain the instinct for action. The slight click of the motel door opening and closing had instantly roused the kid, causing the first shot to miss him widely as he spun off the bed. The second had got him full in the chest as he rushed impulsively through the darkness toward the door.

Boyle stood over him, looking down at the massive wound, then at the zigzag scar below. It was a good-sized scar, although smaller than the one Boyle had carried on his left thigh after World War II. Then it had been as big as a saucer, textured like a nubbed carpet, but with time it had shrunk to the size of a half-dollar, smooth as a birthmark.

Boyle turned away from the body, chilled for a moment by this irony: Warren Shore had survived combat in Vietnam only to die without even time for fear, naked and weaponless, in a California motel room. The moment passed, and Boyle began a systematic search, finding only a small duffel bag which contained a few clothes and enough medicines to stock a drugstore, and in the kid's pants more than nine hundred dollars in cash. That was all. He found the car key on the dresser, went out into the cloudless night, and checked the kid's rented Chevy. Returning to the room, he sat down wearily on the bed and wondered where in the hell the kid had stashed the stolen goods. Finally he got up sluggishly and slipped a small glassine package under the pillow. That would satisfy the cops.

With a last glance at the body, which seemed even smaller in death, Boyle stepped over it and left the room. In his car he lit a cigarette and puffed thoughtfully. Then he started the car and drove away at the dilatory pace of a man exhausted from an assignation. The kid hadn't brought the goods to San Diego, but Boyle had a hunch now who did have them.

In the San Francisco airport, Boyle made three phone calls, the first to Hirschorn. After explaining what had happened in San Diego, he assured Hirschorn that he had a lead on the missing goods. "But I need something," he said. "Get me some knockout drops, something tastless, and send them by messenger to my gallery. No, Allen, not *that* kind. Just a soporific."

Then he called the gallery. "Mr. Vertrees? I'm back in town. Yes, it was shorter than I expected. Did you call Kawabata? What? You couldn't understand her? Come on, his wife speaks better English than we do. Kawabata's drunk, she's just protecting him. No, forget it. I'll go over there myself. Anything going on? Phillips bought it? The red one, four by six? Good. See you in an hour."

Then he phoned Julie Saunders, whose answering service said she would return the call later.

When Boyle arrived at the gallery, his assistant was showing gouaches to a stout woman in a flowered hat. Nodding pleasantly to them, Boyle went into his office and shut the door. He sank down wearily in his swivel chair. The room with its paintings and sculpture looked strange to him, after the blood-spattered room that only last night he had killed a man in. In his youth, swift changes of scene hadn't mattered, but now they tired and often confused him. Cora had warned him this would happen.

The phone rang, he grabbed it quickly, expecting Julie Saunders. But it was Mr. Phillips, wanting to change his purchase from the red to the predominately orange painting. The orange was worth an additional two hundred dollars, so they had a short but lively discussion of price until Phillips, unsuccessful in his haggling, decided to keep the red. Then Vertrees came in, scowling from a long, fruitless session with the stout lady. This was a good excuse for generously giving him the rest of the day off—Boyle wanted him out of the office when Julie Saunders called. Vertrees was too preoccupied to thank his boss, but rushed out like the embattled lover he was. Watching him, Boyle felt a pang of envy.

He picked up *Art News* and was thumbing through it when the phone rang again. This time it was Julie Saunders, her voice thin and wary. See him again? About the guy at the zoo? No? Her voice assumed a cheerful, relaxed tone. Sure she would see him, only not until late, because she had an evening job in Palo Alto. "It's not what you think," she added quickly. "They want a few night shots in front of the university. Could I call you when I get back in town?"

So it was arranged. Boyle sat back then in the chair, his feet on the desk, and fell into a heavy slumber from which

53

he awoke at the sound of the front bell. It was the messenger from Hirschorn.

On his way home Boyle stopped at the Kawabata studio. Mrs. Kawabata opened the door, her face smiling and round as a plate. Bowing low, she gestured him in, murmuring, "Ah, yes, Mr. Broyle."

Boyle glanced quickly around the large atelier, brightly lit by overhead fluorescents. Stacked against the walls were huge canvases, all of them empty save one on which slabs of chrome yellow and apricot, scorched with terra sienna, vibrated tumultuously. It was an abstract painting of astonishing kinetic power, Boyle thought, but he had seen it a month ago, propped in exactly the same position alongside all of those blank canvases. Mrs. Kawabata was guiding him toward a low lacquered table and pillows.

Boyle halted. "Where is he, Mrs. Kawabata?"

Her face puckered in a frown as if she were listening to a language she didn't understand.

"Where is Kenzo?" He glared at a far screen, concealing a tiny corner where he knew a small, frail, wrinkled man was huddling with a glass of whiskey in his hand.

"Kenzo gone," she said with a broad smile, dipping her head a little, like a bird drinking.

"Where is he, Mrs. Kawabata?"

The woman was squat and plump, looking uncomfortable in jeans. Boyle had always seen her in a kimono, and he wondered now if she, like her husband, was succumbing to the blandishments of California life.

"Where?" he repeated.

"He gone with good friend." Her English was much better than this, but Boyle realized helplessly that all he would get out of her today was a few maddeningly vague phrases. "I make tea," she said with a smile and turned to hurry away.

"Wait," Boyle said. "Tell him," his voice rose for the benefit of the man crouching behind the screen, "that I want those paintings by the end of the month or I'm dropping him. Tell him we have a contract, and I intend to see he honors it. Tell him he has the moral responsibility to practice his art. Tell him—" Boyle saw with dismay and frustration that the woman was smiling broadly. Boyle knew and the woman knew and the man behind the screen knew that the paintings would not be finished by the end of the month, possibly not even started, but Kenzo Kawabata would not be dropped from the Boyle Gallery and sooner or later, whiskey or no whiskey, a row of brilliant paintings would hang on the gallery walls, sell out, and command ecstatic reviews. "Tell him," muttered Boyle as he turned on his heel and started for the door, "to *get to work.*"

Outside on the street Boyle ran his fingers nervously through thinning hair. A bitterly amusing idea occurred to him: Perhaps it was easier to kill a thief than to persuade an artist.

He stopped at a liquor store for a bottle of champagne, then bought a pizza with anchovies and sausage, and with it warm beside him on the seat of the car, drove home. Before eating, he called Julie Saunders' answering service and gave his home phone number. Then setting a can of Tab (this was his concession to the diet) on the kitchen table, he opened the cardboard box and attacked the pizza. It was only eight o'clock when he finished, so he took a long, stinging-hot shower, and shaved with great care. He put on a tan suit, candy-striped shirt, and spent an inordinate amount of time selecting a tie to match. By then it was painfully obvious that he wanted to impress Julie Saunders, and not only because his job required it, but also because she was an attractive girl. He disliked his unprofessional attitude. It was no longer easy for him to separate one role from another. In the old days he had been a loving husband one moment and the next, an emotionless professional. Cora had warned him this would happen if he persisted in living two lives. On her deathbed she had stared at him from her large dark eyes, and with her hand trembling in his, had told him he must choose. "You're too old, Alex, for so much change." She had been right, of course, but now when he had a life of calm accomplishment in his grasp, at the first temptation he let it go and rushed back to the old ways. Sitting on the couch, he grimly scanned the room filled with the sculpture and painting his artists had given him. This is what he had always wanted, a life of modest acquisition and peaceful contemplation of mankind's noblest inspirations, and yet within two days he had killed two men. Suddenly in a moment of clear decision, he smacked his fist against his palm of his other hand and vowed that this was the final job.

The phone rang. He leaped for it.

"I'll be there in half an hour," he said.

She lived near the Presidio on Laurel Street in a modern building. Her apartment was filled with overstuffed furniture, throw-cushions, and heavy drapery, all in a muted-blue motif, lit by a single Tiffany lamp. There was a muffling Levantine quality to the room, as if it were a place found in the dark alley of a suk. The effect was faintly sleazy, but exciting, an encouragement of intimacy. Julie seemed to intuit the impression her apartment made on Boyle, because she waved her hand and observed nonchalantly, "They like it." It was her use of "they" that interested him. She felt the need to confess, to flaunt her way of life and test his response, his tolerance. No matter how thoroughly she might rationalize her behavior, no matter how defiantly she gave herself for pay, somewhere in her mind was still the little girl who disobeyed her parents but wanted their sympathy. In spite of the sweet incense pervading the room, in spite of her seductively loose sari-type gown, under which she was obviously naked, Julie Saunders was a blue-eyed American blonde unfit for Middle Eastern practicality.

She left him a moment to put the champagne he had brought into the refrigerator. Another thing about her use of "they"—it set him apart from clients and subtly informed him that he was here on a different basis. She returned from the kitchen with two glasses of Scotch and when he sat down on a couch, she sprawled in front of him on a red cushion, which contrasted brilliantly with the canary color of her gown. Boyle was flattered by her obvious desire to impress him.

She led the conversation, as the dusky light fell across her rather high-cheeked face, giving it soft shadows, a sultry warmth that must have thrilled the blood of many a middle-aged businessman. She talked with enthusiasm of places she wanted to see: Tokyo, Hong Kong, Calcutta, Casablanca. She had read the travel books with the eagerness and naiveté of a retired schoolteacher bound for a first trip abroad. He was touched by her girlish pleasure in a daydream and found himself, against his will, being drawn deeper into her presence. It was Julie who introduced the topic that he should have been waiting impatiently to get to.

"What about that guy?" she asked suddenly, looking at him with a frown.

"Oh, I gave up. I couldn't locate him, so I'll just wait and see if he calls himself."

"That's what I would do." She whirled the ice in her glass, a nervous habit already familiar to him. "So you really didn't come here to talk about him?"

"Of course not." Now was the time to pursue it, but he could only sit there, absorbing the look of her in that hushed, soothing light.

"Why did you come then?"

"I told you. To see you."

"Yes, I believe that," she said gravely. "Only—I don't know."

Boyle failed to react, although her remark was obviously calculated to get a more definite response.

"Shall we have your champagne?"

"Let's let it chill awhile."

"I get the feeling you're not here just to see me."

"That's strange. Why?"

"By now I know something about men," she said with a rueful laugh.

"What did you think I came for?"

"I don't know, but last time I saw you I didn't get the impression you wanted to see me again." After a thoughtful pause, she added, "You seemed more interested in the guy at the zoo."

This was a chance he couldn't afford to lose. She had opened up the subject that would make his own interest in Warren Shore natural. "The truth is," he said, "I got more interested in him the longer I was with you."

"You've lost me."

"I got jealous."

When she laughed, Boyle said, "I mean it. Does it sound so ridiculous?"

"Of course it does! Jealous of what?"

"Of him. I was sure you two were closer than you let on."

For a moment she studied him gravely, then broke into a cheerful smile. "It's corny to be jealous of anyone, but somehow in you I like it."

"Well? Did I have a reason?"

"You've got to be putting me on. I told you, I met him at the zoo, and that was that."

At least she sounded convincing, and he mustn't arouse her suspicion by pursuing this line of argument. With sudden passion he hoped that Julie Saunders was telling the truth, because if she wasn't, he would have to kill her.

"Come here," she murmured.

58

In the next moment he was kneeling beside the cushion, her face warm in the cradle of his hands, and he tried, without wholly succeeding, to forget his job.

They were lying side by side on the deep carpet, her hand resting on his chest.

"It's strange," he said.

"Don't worry. It happens."

She moved her face between his shoulder and neck, burying her eyes. It was like her, he thought, to spare him a direct look.

"I've been tired lately," he said.

"Don't talk about it," she whispered.

She was right, he knew, and probably this happened often with her clients, and because of her sexual experience, probably she didn't care that much. He understood with a mixture of delight, surprise, and dismay that the girl really liked him. Why had he failed? He had wanted her, but between the desire and the act had risen the specters of two men recently killed, then the nightmare image of *her* lying sprawled in a pool of her own blood. He was becoming amateurish as a man and as a professional! In his youth he had gone from the most sordid business to the beds of women. In the days of his marriage he had returned from the nastiest of jobs to Cora without a qualm. Now he was like a seminary student enduring a first experience.

"How about the champagne," he asked her, stirring slightly.

"Wonderful idea!"

He got up naked, wondering if she found his middle-aged body unattractive even as he was wondering if he should do now what he had come to do. He picked up his pants and pulled them on, which made her giggle. "Are you one of those men who hate to be looked at?"

He didn't answer, but moved toward the kitchen, hearing

59

her say in a bright, clear voice, "Well, I *like* the way you look!"

In the kitchen he removed the champagne from the refrigerator, took two glasses from a cabinet, placed them on a table, and from the vial in his pants pocket he poured four or five drops of clear liquid into one of the glasses. Then he popped the cork on the champagne. From the other room he heard her cry out, "Oh, I thought you'd do that in here!" He filled the glasses and carried them into the dimly lit room, knelt beside her, and offered her the drink.

She touched his glass in a toast, but merely sipped the champagne.

"Drink up."

"All right, but don't *you* drink too much. We don't want to have trouble again."

He watched her empty the glass and stretch out happily, asking him with her eyes if he was ready. Boyle raised his own glass and sipped, as though he didn't notice. He began to talk of places he had seen, places that she had been giving her body to see: Chartres with its spired cathedral dominating the farmland, Hampton Court and its pond filled with water-lilies, Berlin, the bazaar at Tunis, Athens, Rome. He spoke in a muted tone, purposefully hypnotic, as he waited for the drug to take effect, and sure enough, her face began to relax, her eyelids fluttered.

"Listen," she said thickly, "I think I'm the one who's tired."

In another minute she was deep in a drugged sleep. Boyle went about his search with methodical care, because if he didn't find the stolen property, he didn't want to leave any trace of what he had done. For three hours he went through everything in the apartment, his fingers briskly skillful as they turned over and then replaced her folded clothes, as they traveled lightly into drawers and closets, probing and leaving, sensing like electronic beams. It was a difficult job because the rooms were cluttered with bric-a-brac, with oddments collected no doubt from the serendipitous little stores of North Beach. Whatever had come the girl's way had been saved, as if she meant to remain here forever. Odd of a girl who dreamed of travel, and yet perhaps such hoarding signified the real Julie Saunders, who unknown even to herself wanted a secure nest, a husband and children, a calm life with only a brave memory of her rebellious past, of her secret adventure. When finally he finished searching, Boyle sat down on the couch to think. He gawked at the sleeping girl, unable to believe he had failed in his lovemaking with her. Was it a measure of his emotional involvement? Perhaps if he had suppressed his feelings for her in the first place, he wouldn't have mistrusted her. He could now assume that Warren Shore hadn't known her at all, aside from their casual meeting at the zoo. Certainly the boy hadn't known her well enough to leave the goods with her, although it was still possible that she had stashed them elsewhere. It was *still possible*. Under the circumstances he could not rule out the possibility of her having tricked him even now. He reviewed the evening like a dog worrying a bone. Had the girl tried to seduce him to disarm him? It was still possible, and there were men he respected who would consider it probable. Sex could make a fool of the best professional. Boyle asked himself then if he would have eliminated her had he found the goods in her apartment. It was the sort of question he wouldn't have asked in his youth, but it was a question he was still professional enough to answer *affirmatively*. Thank God it was now academic.

With a sigh he rose and dressed, having carried out the search in nothing but his pants. He tied his tie in front of the bathroom mirror, glancing with a sense of warmth and delight at the cosmetics lined up on the shelves, at the little personal things which the girl touched each day, all of them suggesting the rituals that prepared her to meet the world. He was getting terribly sentimental and knew it, yet he

61

couldn't help feeling the desire to protect this defiant but troubled girl.

He returned to the living room and studied her sleeping. One nude hip in the glowing air. Her hair fanned out. Her lips slightly parted.

A rush of tenderness had him bending over her, touching her thin bare arm. But that was all. He straightened up, determined not to leave a note for her, though in his mind he composed it: "I guess we were both tired. Love. Alex." He would not, could not leave such a note, which would keep the door open for a further relationship. He couldn't allow her to complicate his life, especially not now, when his entire energy was needed for possibly the most difficult job of a lifetime.

Boyle walked to the door, then turned, and his last glimpse of her shook him in a way only Cora's naked body had ever done. He stared with the awed intensity of a young man, then shut the door quietly behind him, and walked rapidly away. Out in the street, with the first glow of a new day seeping over the roofs of the city, he left the spell of her tacky but oddly charming apartment behind. With a conscious effort he shoved her image out of his mind and became the Sanitation Man again.

The point was, his encounter with Julie Saunders had done no more than eliminate her as a suspect—or rather as a prime suspect. It was still possible that she had tricked him, and he mustn't forget it in the aftermath of his feelings of tenderness. Boyle strode to his car, himself again. Now that he must begin anew, he had the next move to consider.

4

On the morning following his last call from Imperial
Beach, Warren's Aunt Victoria phoned his room time and
again, armed with the baleful knowledge that a hangover
usually kept him in bed until noon. Anxiety prompted her to
contact the motel, and with her nephew's phone call last
evening still in mind, she demanded that the manager check
his room. The manager never called back, so she continued,
with increasing fear, to phone. When a man finally answered, he insisted that she give her name and address before informing her of Warren Shore's death.

She collapsed in a chair as if poleaxed. She had not yet
assimilated this news when there was a knock at the door,
which diverted her from a whirl of images—Warren at the
beach, Warren blowing his nose, Warren pale and drawn in
the VA hospital bed, Warren the baby cradled in her arms,
Warren burying his head against her lap at the news of his
parents' death, Warren smiling at the brilliant sight of the
Golden Gate Bridge—and fixed her attention upon the shaft
of sunbeams lying across the door, the day having pro-
gressed into afternoon. The caller was a detective from the
San Francisco force, acting in behalf of the San Diego police.

63

Through him she learned that a packet of heroin had been found under Warren's pillow. His questioning of her was crude, bludgeoning, an insistent attempt at eliciting from her any sort of information that would confirm the police theory of a drug-associated murder. Time and again he came back to the fact that Warren had been a war veteran.

"My nephew and heroin? Never!" she declared and met the cool blue-eyed stare of the detective with an unwavering stare of her own. It was obvious that the police were convinced and from the hammering but mechanical questioning, it was obvious that they viewed this as another routine crime of the sort Victoria heard reported over TV in the evenings.

"Not my nephew," she repeated at the door, so angry at the man's blindly arrogant manner that she didn't even point out what to *her* was obvious: Someone could have put the heroin in the motel room solely for this purpose—to fool the police. Had the man been halfway sympathetic, she probably would have told him about the bus that Warren had robbed, but alone in the afternoon shadows, she was glad that she'd kept silent. Warren's foolish act would have merely confirmed the detective's suspicion—a young war veteran, hooked on drugs in Vietnam, committed robberies to support his habit. That detective with his square-jawed face, his crew cut, his ice-blue eyes would have discounted her wild claim that Warren Shore had robbed a busload of dead people. Possibly with companions he had robbed the passengers, then sent the bus over the Coast Road, because that was logical, a hard fact the hard detective and his kind could accept.

Victoria Welch sat there in the waning afternoon, her suspicion growing that Warren had been marked for murder from the moment he robbed the bus. Only three days ago, when he came to her apartment hauling a laundry bag full of stolen goods and begging her to hold it for him, she had warned him of trouble, not merely because he had committed a crime, but because the circumstances were so bizarre. Warren had laughed at her fears, which seemed to him based upon superstition—robbing the dead, that sort of thing—and he had argued that no one could possibly trace him. He shrugged when she suggested that the dead passengers had been shoved over the cliff to make their deaths appear accidental. Doubtlessly when he shrugged, Warren was dreaming of the zoo he was going to see. But how had they been killed? she persisted. He had a ready if disinterested answer: by gas fumes from a defective engine. It was even possible, he added with a touch of flippancy, that the bus driver had driven them over the cliff in order to save the company embarrassment. And she countered by asking why the driver hadn't also been gassed, or, if he had escaped that, why had he been found in the wrecked bus along with the passengers? Again Warren shrugged, gazing out the window, having no further interest in the matter. It wasn't that he lacked imagination; his was simply occupied elsewhere: in the fantasy world he had escaped to ever since coming home from Vietnam. Three days ago he had wanted only one thing and that was to see those animals in the San Diego Zoo.

Poor Warren, he'd never had any luck: losing his parents at twelve, going to a war he didn't believe in, suffering from a painful wound and enduring a long rehabilitation. He'd never had the chance to find himself. It was unfair. It was unjust. It was disgraceful that this unlucky young man, who had sacrificed so much for his country, must go dishonored to an early grave.

Warren, dead. Her nephew. *Someone had murdered him.*

That fact brought her to the edge of her chair.

Someone had murdered him because of the bus.

She brought her hands together in a furious steeple of concentration, as she remembered Warren saying that a man had been following him. She got up and began pacing, irritably adjusting the glasses on her nose.

Someone had murdered Warren because of the bus.

Shadows lengthened, the soft light dimmed to lavender and then faded, but she continued to pace without turning a lamp on. In the darkness her mind focused on a single idea: Warren had been killed because he robbed that bus.

If only her husband were alive, he would sort the facts out, he would defend Warren's name. Warren a dope addict? Never! It was unfair, unjust, disgraceful that the police considered him a dope addict merely because he had fought for his country. Her nephew another cipher in the crime statistics? Never!

Victoria halted and whipped her glasses off, as if she were a man preparing to enter a street fight. Henry was no longer here to do the thinking, to take charge, but just the same, Warren's killer must be brought to justice. So *she* would see to it. With the last breath of her body she would fight to clear her nephew's name. What would Henry tell her to do? Just that. What she had especially admired in her husband was his Old World sense of honor. As a couple they had been an island in a sea of cynicism, and now as an individual she must bear witness to the truth of the verities they had believed in together. Yes!

Turning the lights on, Victoria went into the kitchen to make tea. Her hands were trembling. She could trace her forbears back to the pioneers who fought and died on the westering trails. In those days people took care of their own, and that was fitting, and today, in a world of jaded policemen for whom justice was mechanical duty, it was fitting that she, Warren's only relative, should defend his reputation. God knows, few people had paid attention to him in his short life. She watched the first bubbles rise to the surface of the heating water.

In a wild moment of impulse he had taken the personal effects of dead people, which was a dismaying thing to do, but he had been in a terrible war and though his body had recovered, his mind had still been suffering from it. But a

66

dope addict? Never! If there was one thing in the world that she detested, it was drug addiction. When she heard the words, certain images flashed into her mind: schoolchildren strolling home from school, accosted by a grinning, sleazy man; dark alleys and the glint of needles; a slavering girl tied down to a hospital bed. Her Warren a dope fiend? Never!

Into a pot she measured four teaspoonfuls of Ching Wo, a special Chinese black, and then with a decisive shrug of her shoulders, strode into the other room and called old Sackman. She explained rapidly in an inflectionless voice that her nephew had died in San Diego, that she must go down there for a few days to settle affairs. The news came so unexpectedly, so starkly, that the chief librarian was too flustered—or perhaps too slow-witted, Victoria thought—to ask embarrassing questions. The call was finished in a couple of minutes and Victoria went back to the brewing. After her crisp handling of old Sackman, the Ching Wo's aroma seemed to her especially subtle.

As she sipped, Victoria told herself once more that she was going to find her nephew's murderer. It was a resolution that both thrilled and rattled her. But there was no time to dwell on the patent bravado of such an idea—she must go at it and go at it logically, step by step, like the sleuths in mysteries. She must begin with what she had—the property itself. So Victoria got up and hauled the laundry bag out of the closet—stunned for a moment by the realization that the detective could easily have found it. She could imagine the ensuing events: She branded as the accomplice of her dope fiend nephew; the trial; her incarceration; Sackman crowing in the background.

Victoria upturned the bag and dumped everything out on the floor. Scattered around her, as she got down with difficulty on her knees, was an assortment of the common things people carry. But these things were somehow special, because someone had murdered her nephew because of

67

them. If her investigation (*her* investigation!) followed the standard rules of detection she had encountered in detective stories, the objects here ought to provide clues. Old Sackman had always ridiculed her enthusiasm for thrillers, and it certainly was true that she loved a good mystery, the twists and turns, the false starts, the buried clue, the sudden sky-bright solution. The chief librarian's scorn had never bothered her, and now less than ever. Let the old bat laugh. Victoria figured that years of such reading had provided her with scraps of knowledge she could apply now to a *real* case in which the verities of justice and honor were actually at stake. Looking at the wallets and jewelry spread before her, like so many pieces of the kind of crossword puzzle she worked each Sunday, Victoria resolved to analyze them by using the traditions of logic and intuition that had served Holmes and Dupin so well. Or at least she was going to try.

Born under Aquarius, the same sign as Darwin and Galileo, she was determined to go about her investigation scientifically, without jumping to conclusions. She began therefore with an analysis of the stolen property. Did its character reveal anything? Was there something about one or all of the objects spread before her that conveyed a special meaning? She put the watches in one pile, jewelry in another, wallets in a third, and miscellaneous objects in a fourth. After long scrutiny of each item, Victoria decided that the most striking thing about all of this property was its *unexceptional* character. No valuable stones, no solid gold or platinum gewgaws, this was stuff belonging to the hard-working middle-class: functional, commonplace, worn or carried with protective pride.

Next, from names in wallets and engravings on jewelry, she made an alphabetical list, ranging from Allen to Weller. She studied the names for a pattern that would bind them together, familially or racially. She rather expected to find a preponderance of Italians, recent books and movies having associated them clearly in her mind with violence. But the names were predominantly English, with a liberal sprinkling of Germans and Chinese, as well as Italians, along with a few Middle Europeans and one Latin.

The most important aspect of the examination would now begin. Before starting it, Victoria got herself another cup of Ching Wo and stretched to relieve the backache which had developed from her staying in a hunched position so long. She had been in a housecoat and her favorite frayed slippers all day. This was her Sunday outfit, worn when she had the leisure for good tea and good books and a special program on television, and time to stand at the window and watch with nostalgia the couples strolling toward Fisherman's Wharf.

She gathered together all the identity papers, credit cards, and snapshots from the wallets, and piled them on the desk. On a large sheet of ruled paper she listed the passengers down the left side and across the top she wrote four headings: Age, Address, Occupation, Organizations. With the fastidious care of a skilled librarian, she examined each document and entered appropriate information under the proper category. Once this was done, she analyzed the data. It was clear that most of the passengers were elderly, their median age being fifty-three, although a half-dozen of them were under thirty. Nearly all of them were from San Diego and nearby communities: La Mesa, Lemon Grove, National City, Paradise Hills. She was disappointed by the variety of occupations, which ranged from nurse and engineer to aircraft worker and barber. She assumed that those who had no occupational identification were housewives and retired people. She had placed her highest hope in the organizations, but here too she was frustrated. What she found was a number of different affiliations with unions and guilds, health and credit organizations, the impersonal data of a computer world. Finally, her perusal of snapshots confirmed her assumption that these people had lived commonplace, orderly, decent lives. Most of the photos were of small children or young mothers holding babies or pretty girls posed on lawns and beaches or white-haired couples standing in front of modest homes.

Victoria shoved the papers aside and propped her elbows on the desk, listening fitfully to the shrill cry of gulls from the waterfront. Then she took a news clipping from the desk drawer and reread it. This was an account of the bus accident, not more than fifteen lines, which stated that a San Diego bus returning from a tour of the western states had plunged from the Coast Road. Her labyrinthine detection had uncovered no more than that, she realized ruefully. Her great effort had merely confirmed what the article said: The bus was from San Diego and carried tourists. And the account added one bit of information unavailable from the pile of objects: the name of the bus company.

She and Edna Sutton had been friends since childhood. Edna was a Libra with her moon in Leo, and true to such an astrological combination she was tall and slim, possessing the ethereal features of someone devoted to the spiritual life. She was an artistic Libra whose moon encouraged generosity, but the two signs also combined to make her somewhat gullible and an easy prey to flattery. She and Victoria had been widowed the same year and once they had taken a pleasant trip together through Mexico. Of the dozen people Victoria knew in San Diego, she chose to call this old friend for help.

No sooner had Edna answered the phone than Victor'a told her bluntly of Warren's death, of the heroin in the motel room, of the unfair assumptions made by the police. Victoria did not, however, mention the bus robbery—the stars had blessed her with a more cautious nature than Edna's.

At the end of this brisk account, Edna began to sob and lament, "Oh, Vicky, oh, Vicky," and Victoria could imagine the thin, high-cheeked face, the large staring eyes, the pale and trembling lips. Victoria waited for the heartfelt outburst to subside, then in a crisp voice reserved for conferring with researchers in the library, she announced that tomorrow she was taking a bus tour.

"What, Vicky? A—bus tour?" The lament was suddenly replaced by shocked incredulity. "Vicky, *what* did you say?"

"Tomorrow, I'm taking a bus from San Diego. The Western Tour Line."

"Then you'll be here tomorrow? For the funeral?"

"Let me explain, Edna. I'm not coming to San Diego for the funeral. I'm coming to catch a bus in connection with Warren's murder. *Do* you understand?"

"Oh, Vicky." The voice shook from bewilderment, grief—Edna had known Warren, had found no difficulty in loving him as she loved her friend.

"Edna, there's something I want you to do for me."

"Anything!"

Victoria was going to upset poor Edna even more with this request: She wanted Edna to arrange for Warren's cremation, and not only that, but for "a plane burial" as well. Shortly after Warren had left the hospital, he had arrived at Victoria's apartment one evening, drunk, muttering about death. He had sat on the couch, gulping the Scotch she kept for visitors and Christmas, declaring that when he died he wanted to be cremated and his ashes scattered from a plane over the Pacific. How like him that was! And Victoria had solemnly sworn, at his insistence that evening, to arrange for his disposal in exactly this manner should he die before her. She had agreed, perhaps, because she never dreamed she would survive him. Now her promise must be kept. She explained this to Edna, whose response was a quick intake of breath, a whispered "Vicky."

"Will you make these arrangements, Edna?"

"Of course," her friend replied instantly. "But won't you be here at all?"

71

"It's *vital* I get the bus tomorrow. Another doesn't leave for three days. I *must* do it, Edna."

"If you must, you must. Of course I'll arrange things. But I don't understand—"

"Someday, when there's time, I'll explain it all." Victoria glanced down at her watch, a Longine which was the last gift her husband had ever given her, with the engraving on the back: *To My Dear Wife.* "Edna, I have to get ready, *now*. Packing, reservations, and tomorrow before leaving here, I must go to the bank." Again the image rose in her mind: the thin face, the luminous eyes, the pale lips tight from tension. "Dear friend," said Victoria gently, "please don't judge me."

"I won't. I never have. Do what you must do, and I'll do my own part."

And Edna would; Victoria could count on it. Loyal Edna would arrange for the strange funeral, so distasteful to her own beliefs, as if a scattering of ashes over the ocean was the purest way of joining God, as if Warren were her own flesh and blood and his views were hers. Victoria plummeted down in a chair after this phone call, giving herself to old memories of Warren, then of Edna in Mexico, face beatific at the first sight of Popocatepetl—how vulnerable a woman of sixty was to images of the past! She roused herself and first called an airline, then the Western Tour Busline in San Diego. There was plenty to do before she slept, there was no time for the luxury of brief. All her life Victoria Welch had faced calamity and misfortune in this forthright manner, with dogged self-control. Even when the worst had happened—her husband keeling over one afternoon from a heart seizure—her response had been immediate, practical, and in better circumstances might have saved his life. Within seconds of his collapse, she had been down on her knees, giving him mouth-to-mouth resuscitation, pounding his chest with a fist as resolute as a man's in an effort to stimulate heart action. For some people this mastery of her feel-

72

ings had been cold-blooded; they had been astonished and ultimately displeased by an otherwise compliant little woman's toughness of mind. They didn't understand that although someone like chief librarian Sackman might walk all over her when the issue was petty, let a crisis come along and Victoria Welch was prepared to face it with her sun in Aquarius and her moon in Aries, putting her faith in clear thought, immediate action, and a strong will.

A single question hammered away at Alexander Boyle as he sat in his office with the door shut: *Where had the kid stashed those goods?* It seemed probable now that Shore had left them with someone other than Julie Saunders before heading south to the zoo. Shore had plenty of cash for the trip, so there was no reason for carting the property around. But if he hadn't left it with Julie, then with someone in the sleazy North Beach hotel? That was unlikely, because hotels of that sort were about as safe as Market Street at midnight. On the evidence of the kid's notebook and from what Boyle had seen of his behavior, he had been paranoid as well as obsessive, a combination suggesting that he would count only on someone he had completely trusted in the past. This could be a girl, an army buddy, possibly a relative. Because of his irascible character, however, it was doubtful that Shore had made friends easily in the service or after his discharge formed a solid relationship with a girl. But what sort of relative would accept for safekeeping a bagful of watches and jewelry, without being suspicious? Only someone who was crooked, foolish, or submissive.

And so Boyle came back full circle to the question, pursuing it like a chipmunk on a treadmill. He pulled out the notebook, hoping that another look at it might provide a new direction, and he was turning the pages slowly, when the phone rang. He got up, opened the door, and called Mr. Vertrees, who was sitting with a magazine in the gallery.

"If it's Miss Saunders," Boyle instructed him, "I'm out."

With a smirk the lean young man ambled into the office and answered the phone. "Boyle Gallery. Yes? Who is calling, please? I see. Yes. Well, I'm sorry but he's out. No, I don't know when. Would you care to leave your number? I see. At any rate, I'll tell him you called." Mr. Vertrees replaced the phone, met Boyle's eyes briefly, and without a word returned to the gallery, closing the office door behind him.

Shaking off the recollection of incense, red cushions, and soft white skin, Boyle picked up the notebook again. He flipped pages until coming to the phone numbers. Of course! He had forgotten all about the library number with its smudged extension. Why would a restless, confused kid like Warren Shore write down the number of a library? He was hardly the type to spend his days studying at a desk or prowling the stacks. He'd had a livelier place to prowl.

It was a slim hope, but Alexander Boyle was ready to grasp at anything. He opened the office door and told Vertrees he was going out.

Miss Sackman, chief librarian. Hers was the first of nine extensions beginning with the number three.

He waited in a cramped but immaculate little office for almost ten minutes before a small, elderly woman swept in, her mouth already working. "I am sorry you had to wait, sir, I'm dreadfully busy today with everyone out for one reason or other it leaves me with everything to do can I help you?" The little woman, perhaps in her mid-sixties, wore a rumpled print frock of a raucous color too youthful for her, heavy rouge, and a brown hairpiece that mismatched the essential gray of her own hair. Without waiting for his reply, she continued. "People think we have nothing to do but sit around reading books. Books! Ha! I never have time for them it seems and yet people look at me dumbfounded when I say I haven't even opened the latest bestseller. Sir?"

Boyle opened his wallet and held out a private investigator's card. Miss Sackman swung up a pair of glasses that dangled from her neck on a leather cord. She studied Boyle's fake identification judiciously. "When I heard who you were from Miss Claremont I couldn't believe it I said to myself what could a man like that want with me but here you are, aren't you? Please sit *down*," she enthused, plumping her own considerable bulk into a swivel chair behind a desk without one scrap of paper on it. "It isn't every day we have investigators here don't you know. It's a regimented life we lead but a taxing one you may be sure although people think we have nothing better to do all day than read read read. But I avoid novels on principle. Do you?" She chuckled and waved her hand expansively. "But obviously you've come for information isn't that right? Is it about one of our periodical readers?"

Boyle was thinking of a reply when she added, "You can *confide* in me, sir. When it comes to a confidence, I'm a tomb." She leaned forward, her face beaming from the anticipated pleasure of collaboration. "People think I don't know what is going on in this place they see me bustling here and there and think well she's too busy to notice. But I never miss a single solitary thing and between us I suspect more than one of them. I'm talking about those periodical readers."

"Miss Sackman—"

"The way they come off the street and sit all day with a magazine—I think look at them they have no idea of reading, they are up to something else. Plotting or something. Of course some just don't have anywhere to go but I have seen many of them I suspected. They are working out something to the detriment of other people or this community. They are if I know anything at all about human nature. I have two things in my favor, sir—strict attention to detail and a knowledge of human nature."

75

"Yes. Miss Sackman, I'm looking for a young man who may be connected in some way with your library and—"

"If he is I'll know it."

"And all I have to go on is his name, so I'd appreciate—"

"Isn't it always the way with you investigators? You start with almost nothing and you *build.* I never was a mystery fan like some people I know." She flicked her hand dismissively. "This responsibility I have here doesn't give me time for that sort of frivolity. I don't even have time for the Sunday paper. On weekends there is so terribly much to do in my own apartment, my lists for example." She gave him a sidelong confidential glance. "Do you make lists, sir? I find them vital. I make a complete list once a week of the contents of my refrigerator," she proudly declared. "That's how I keep my food *fresh,* you see, and let me tell you the people who say they can remember something without making a note of it are just fooling themselves. Order depends on keeping a careful record. My father taught me that. But I'm telling you something you already know because as an investigator you're trained have you made a mental list of everything in my office? See? I know you have!"

"Miss Sackman," Boyle went on quickly while she was stopping for breath, "his name is Shore."

"Shore?" The little woman shook her head emphatically. "No one here by that name."

"Perhaps you'll remember him by his appearance. He has a black beard and wears a long coat—"

"And half the time is blowing his nose. That's her queer nephew."

"Pardon me?"

"Victoria Welch's queer nephew. The only thing she ever told me about him was he was a war hero but if you ask me he looks like one of those soldiers who killed children in Vietnam. Brooding and wild. He looks doped to me and the beard and that coat—"

"Mrs. Welch works here?"

"Miss, although she is widowed and I think it desecrates his memory to use Miss but she thinks it gives her an air of independence. Died just like that." Miss Sackman snapped her fingers. "I'm talking about her husband. But I understand he was overweight—she didn't watch his diet." The little woman peered owlishly at Boyle. "You men must watch your diet because I read in a medical journal it's primarily a man's disease. Whenever I get a chance to read I concentrate on medical journals because that's where the facts are, the *hard facts*. Victoria's my assistant in Circulation because I had to take her out of Reference for keeping her nose in a book in spite of a great deal of personnel resistance, I don't mind telling you. Staff has no idea of the problems of administration. But then so many of them side with her because she was here before me. Poor soul has simply never adjusted to the fact I was hired over her because what's needed in this position is someone with a sense of order. I'm telling you because you're looking for facts, but being a librarian doesn't mean disappearing into the stacks like some people I know to read a book on their own. We have three people in Circulation alone who do that. When I said to—"

"Is she here now?"

The question breaking in on her own train of thought seemed to confuse Miss Sackman momentarily. "Do you mean Victoria Welch? No. She's not."

"Out to lunch?"

"In San Diego where her nephew died suddenly just the night before last I think it was, although with Victoria you can never be sure of the facts. They found him in a motel somewhere I think she said and if *that* isn't suspicious I'd like to know what is. But I gave her time off to go down there and put things in order, poor boy, what did he do?"

Boyle had turned and with a short wave of farewell was leaving the office.

"Is that all?"

"Thank you," Boyle said, opening the door.

77

"What did that boy do?" Miss Sackman started to rise.

"I'm not investigating his death, Miss Sackman."

"Very well," she replied sulkily. "But you tell Victoria Welch and I'm sure you will during your investigation whatever it is if that boy died under suspicious circumstances or had a gun battle with the police or got involved with drugs or rape or anything at all, I'll help her in any way I can. It's my job you see and I—"

Boyle closed the door gently behind him and from a girl at the circulation desk learned where Victoria Welch lived. As he left the library, he caught a last glimpse of the stout little woman, glasses perched on her nose, peering out at him through a crack in her office door.

It was almost three o'clock when he arrived at Victoria Welch's apartment building near Fisherman's Wharf. In the vestibule he found her apartment number and climbed four flights. The dingy hallway was lit by bulbs of small wattage and the pungent odor of fish drifting in from the wharf settled like swamp air along the passage. Somehow he hadn't expected a librarian to live in such a forlorn, unkempt, rugged building. On the fourth floor landing he waited a few moments, listening for sounds from the apartment opposite hers and from the floor overhead. The building was silent. Boyle took a cloth from his pocket and untied it, exposing a half dozen pieces of oiled blue metal in the shape of thin spatulas. On the third try he found a pick that worked, and although he had never been good at picking locks, he managed this one within a minute. He slipped on gloves, entered the apartment, and for the next hour systematically searched the bedroom, living room, and kitchen.

The goods were not there.

Boyle sat down wearily on a couch, absorbing the bitter truth that although he had found nothing, the occupant of this apartment was, with Julie Saunders, the only link he yet had to the goods. That garrulous old librarian, Miss Sackman, had been right about one thing: His investigation would eventually lead him to Victoria Welch. Here in her apartment Boyle had the chance to study her before they met. The furnishings were much like the building, forlorn, rugged, and unkempt. This was a woman who preferred function to aesthetics. The walls were bare save for book-cases and a couple of framed photos. Boyle got up and strolled around, peering at the book titles: Shakespeare, a set of Dickens, histories—what he would expect of a li-brarian—and a full shelf of astrology books, which surprised him. He paused for a long look at two framed photographs of a formally posed middle-aged couple. The man was bald, his face sallow and craggy, and the steel-rimmed glasses he wore gave him a severely judicious expression. The woman was unattractive, her eyes too small and her nose too big, her gray hair frizzled and out of control, and yet her wide, dimpled smile seemed to dominate both of the pictures. Boyle recalled having seen a photo album in the desk, so he got it out and sat down with it in his lap, like a guest prepared to comment favorably on someone's family history. The photos were chronologically arranged, so he skipped early ones of two plump little girls in sandboxes and swings, and moved on to snapshots of two skinny adolescents, pos-sibly Victoria Welch and her sister—Warren Shore's mother? Boyle thumbed swiftly through groups of laughing girls and young couples posed within college arches and on lawns drinking beer, then paused at one of a young couple stand-ing in front of a broad expanse of beach. This had been Victoria Welch in her bloom, a rangy, sportive, shaggy-haired girl in a one-piece bathing suit, her thighs muscled but well-proportioned, her breasts large and firm, obviously coveted by the athletic young man whose powerful arm was draped over her shoulder. He bore no resemblance to the bald man in glasses who appeared in a later photo, his hair already thin, wearing a tux alongside Victoria Welch in a wedding dress. Then came photos of them with other couples on boats or lounging at campsites. Boyle recognized the sister again, grown into a beautiful woman who was accompanied by a different man in almost every snapshot. Finally a small, rather effete-looking man with intense eyes appeared frequently and at last stood beside her in a wedding photo, with Victoria and her own husband ranged on either side. The remainder of the album was devoted principally to snapshots of a baby held by the sister and then to a skinny boy with his father's intense eyes. At a certain point Victoria's husband disappeared from the photos and at another, so did the sister and her husband. A plumper and grayer Victoria Welch was seen observing a boy on a bike, a boy playing tennis in shorts too big for him, a boy leaning out of a car, his mouth set in a grim line. In these photos Warren Shore began to assume more and more distinctly those features that Boyle had last seen lunging toward the motel door. In the album's last snapshot, Victoria Welch held hands with a scowling young soldier in front of the apartment building Boyle had entered an hour ago.

The album told the story with unmistakable clarity. Victoria Welch was a childless widow who had lavished care and affection on an orphaned nephew.

Boyle picked up the phone and called Hirschorn, asking him to get the name of the San Diego funeral home where Warren Shore had been taken on his aunt's request from the morgue. "Let me know at the gallery," Boyle said.

"Are you going back down to San Diego?" Hirschorn asked.

"Looks like it."

"You're sure getting a workout. How's the diet?"

"Ha," Boyle grunted, rang off, and left the apartment.

Boyle was alone in the gallery, putting his affairs in order for the trip in the morning. He spoke by phone to his accountant, a buyer, a reviewer from a local magazine, and a trucking company that specialized in art delivery. When the phone rang, he thought it was Hirschorn calling with the information.

But it was Julie Saunders.

"I called you three times," she declared, "but that assistant of yours wouldn't tell me where you were."

"He didn't know."

"Is he cute?"

"I suspect you'd think so."

"I don't like the sound of your voice."

"Why not?"

"It's cold. Are you angry?"

"Of course not."

"I can't understand why I fell asleep that way. What in hell did you put in the champagne? At least you could have stayed overnight. After all, I'd wake up sooner or later." Her laugh was short, brilliant. "I mean, didn't we have some unfinished business?"

"We certainly did. Look, Julie, please don't blame me. I'm not angry, I'm just damn busy."

"That's what they all say." She was beginning to sound bitter. Next she might cry. Boyle couldn't believe that such an attractive young girl was actually interested in *him*, and for a moment his suspicion flared. Had she already learned of Warren Shore's murder and did she link him to it? But if she thought he was a murderer, would she bring herself so persistently to his attention? Did she have the stolen goods and was she maneuvering to get a nice reward for their return? But if she had them, wouldn't she know they were not worth an elaborate intrigue? It still seemed probable that his only reason for mistrusting Julie Saunders was her apparent interest in him. It took no better student of human nature than chief librarian Sackman to see what really bothered him was the sincerity of the girl's feelings for a middle-aged man.

"Are you still there?" she asked irritably.

"I was thinking—could we get together later in the week?"

"When?" she demanded.

"Well, could I call you?"

"If that's how you want it."

"It's not how I want it, but—"

"Alex, don't play games. If you'd rather not see me again, then simply don't. It's just that right now you're on my mind and I can't help it. I'm making a fool of myself because I'm in love or think I am or whatever the hell it is. Don't say anything. I hate people who force people. I'm going to stop talking now."

"I'll call."

"Good luck, Alex."

"I'll call."

He heard the phone click, and in the ensuing silence Alexander Boyle was convinced of the girl's sincerity. He lit a cigarette and in a happy mood phoned a coffee shop to send him two cheeseburgers with everything and an order of french fries. He had to celebrate *some* way. Not that he ever expected to see her again, but after all, it wasn't every day that a man his age attracted a lovely young woman. So there he was, trusting her. In his work, it was both amateurish and foolhardy to believe in anyone. More than once in the old days he had seen the results of trust: A corpse floating in the bay was only the simplest of consequences.

He was glum by the time a delivery boy came with his order, and for a couple of minutes he let the food cool before eating it. He was halfway through the second cheeseburger when the phone rang again. This time it was Hirschorn with the name of the funeral home. Arrangements had been made for cremation and a scattering of the ashes over the Pacific.

"There's something else you should know," Hirschorn said. "The arrangements weren't made by the kid's aunt. They were made by a Mrs. Edna Sutton."

"Who is?"

"The funeral director said a friend of the family."

"Yes, that's something I should know."

"And another thing: Hopkins is getting itchy. He's not satisfied and won't be until we get the property back."

"You don't have to spell it out."

"I know, but he wanted me to tell you again."

"Tell h'm I'm not up a blind alley yet."

"I know you aren't. Maybe it's our age, Alex. Take my own business, for example. You might not think it makes a difference in real estate, but it does. Clients would rather buy from a young man, so I keep two on hand for meeting the public. What I do is draw up the contracts. Alex, we're getting to the age where people lose confidence in us."

"Just so we don't lose it in ourselves."

"Thatta boy. What should I tell Hopkins?"

"Tell him what I told you—I'm not up a blind alley yet."

"Thatta boy."

But after hanging the phone up, Boyle was not so sure of himself. Initially he had blundered by not checking the bus while Tony Aiello was replacing the fuel line hose, and ever since then he had been stumbling through the darkness with just enough light to keep from losing his way completely. He stared at the half-eaten cheeseburger and disdainfully shoved it away. He had no business breaking his diet because he was anxious or because he was happy. Because he was happy? There was nothing to be happy about. For that matter, Julie Saunders was not altogether out of the woods. What if Shore actually had been her lover, would she revenge herself on his murderer if she could? She had that kind of guts, that kind of passion. Or given her desire for travel money—after all, she sold her body for it—did she see in the commonplace goods a possible chance for blackmail? The circumstances under which Warren Shore had stolen them might suggest to her that they had special value for someone. That could explain why she wasted time on a man old enough to be her father. Boyle grimly imagined her inspecting her savings account week after week and month after month, planning for the day when there were sufficient funds for a jet trip to Hong Kong, a cruise to Calcutta. When he considered the possibilities unemotionally, he had to admit she was not out of the woods at all.

Hesitating for a moment, Boyle picked up the cold cheeseburger and fiercely bolted it. Then he lit another cigarette and inhaled deeply, bitterly aware that his present assignment and the ascetic life were no more compatible than were a man his age and a lovely young girl.

5

So here, incredibly, she was: sitting next to the window, looking across irrigated green fields at distant mountains wrapped in blue haze, while beside her a fat woman was snoring. Victoria glanced at the sleeping Piscean, at the rumpled dress, the ballooning jowls, the capillaries threading the florid, alcoholic face. This was a true Piscean, indulgent and destructive, who had drunk herself into collapse last night in a Yuma restaurant. It had taken Victoria less than a day to learn the astrological signs of all thirty-eight passengers, and this unhappy, fat woman was the only Piscean, which made Victoria think of her poor nephew, who had also been born under that ill-starred sign. Let people laugh—the signs never lied. A wizened old lady in front of Victoria offered her a piece of gum. Ever since their noon departure from San Diego yesterday, the old lady had been besieging everyone with candy and magazines and advice for a healthy trip—a Leo, generous to a fault, too busy with help to recognize her own foolishness. From the middle of the bus Victoria looked over the heads of passengers, excited and flustered by the knowledge that she alone was not what she seemed. Doubtlessly this sense of purposeful alienation from other people was secretly cherished by detectives. Now and then she felt guilty from enjoying a similar thrill, because in a way it was at Warren's expense. Yet she couldn't help feeling pleasure in the exercise of her powers of observation, as she studied the rows of people. People like them must have begun the same journey in the same manner in a similar bus only a few days ago: most of them elderly, a few of them couples with young children, and all of them solid, middle-class citizens who for reasons of money or health had chosen to see the Western states by guided bus tour.

What had those other people seen or done that resulted not only in their sitting dead and upright at dawn on a San Francisco street, but also in their plunging, hours later, over a cliff in an apparent accident? Victoria meant to duplicate those fatal circumstances by taking an identical tour on the same busline, and though it was unlikely that similar events would occur, she might be able to reconstruct what those events had been. If her determination needed shoring up, Victoria had only to glance at the Piscean snoring next to her and the vision of her unlucky nephew leaped to mind.

The fat woman snuffled uncomfortably in her alcoholic sleep. Victoria nearly reached out to stroke her plump, spasmodically tensing hand and allay her fears.

After an hour's cruise on Lake Mead in a sightseeing boat and a short walking tour of Hoover Dam, they returned to the bus. Nearing the parking lot under a cool canopy of evergreens, Victoria made a point of staying close to the driver, who doubled as guide. Deciding to begin her investigation with him, Victoria had been "cultivating" him, to use a term for ingratiation which her mother had taught her, along with "reading" people and avoiding "fast" companions. Victoria "cultivated" the driver by describing the best traits of his sign, Sagittarius: curiosity, forcefulness, a keen sense of humor. On the walk back to the bus, by exploiting his Sagittarian tendency to talk too much, she soon learned that he had worked for the busline a decade, was a father of three, and loved to travel.

"I can guess, too," Victoria told the powerfully built little man, "you are an athlete."

Mr. Carver smiled broadly. "I sure was, when I was a kid. Look at this." He shoved up the blue sleeve of his coat and unbuttoned the cuff of his shirt, revealing a thin scar from wrist to forearm. "These three guys jumped me in Balboa Park last year. One of them cut me, but I had two of them down when the cop arrived. They must've been fifteen years younger than me."

Victoria inspected the scar with appropriate awe, thinking, however, of the far more terrible wound that her nephew had received in Vietnam. She said to Mr. Carver, "I would hate to have the responsibility of protecting the lives of so many people, the way you have."

"I enjoy it," the driver said proudly.

"Well, it certainly can be dangerous."

Mr. Carver slowed his pace and glanced at her. "How's that?"

"Didn't a bus from your line have a terrible accident just a few days ago?"

Mr. Carver's face clouded up, his mouth tightened. "A good friend of mine drove that bus."

"How awful for you."

"First accident we ever had like that. It's hard to believe, let me tell you. You never met a better driver than Paul Reskin." They had reached the bus where Mr. Carver took Victoria's arm to help her up the stairwell. "But don't you worry, Miss Welch. That accident was one in a million."

"Oh, I won't, with you at the wheel." One in a million, she repeated to herself.

On the last leg of the day's journey, Victoria sat alone, the Pisces having moved to an empty row down the aisle. That was typical of a Piscean, typical too of poor Warren, who

87

had always been a loner. But given a little luck and more time, he might have turned his brooding quality of mind to good use.

Victoria was so absorbed by thoughts of her nephew that she failed to see the wrinkled old Leo offer her a chocolate bar. Canyon walls in the distance were struck afire by the sunset, and the lustrous color seemed to quicken her blood, to lift her resolve toward a new height of surety. When finally she noticed the candy bar, she took it with such profuse and emphatic thanks that the old woman gawked at her.

The bus arrived in Las Vegas after dark, the twinkling lights of the city like a cluster of fireflies on the dark plain. Mr. Carver announced over the mike that people interested in a tour of the casinos and nightclubs should assemble at nine o'clock in front of the bus. Those exhausted by the day or unwilling to spend extra money chose to remain behind for a quiet dinner at the motel restaurant, then bed or a stroll. Victoria stayed behind, but for neither of those reasons. Victoria resolved to keep her psychic forces marshalled, like a chess master on the eve of a contest, or Sherlock Holmes who, to the exasperated amazement of Dr. Watson, hoarded his energy during a case by taking catnaps. So Victoria got into pajamas—she hadn't worn a nightgown since her husband's death and had shocked a local welfare organization by contributing to them a half-dozen black and red and pink negligees of the sheerest silk, picking up each almost weightless fabric in a mottled hand and grinning at it in frankly erotic memory—put on her housecoat, and watched the news on television. Then she fluffed the pillows and began her fourth reading of *Crime and Punishment*. At the end of the first chapter, Victoria put the book aside and placed a call to San Diego. By then Edna would have returned from her Saturday night bridge club, an event she never missed.

There had been plane trouble, so Warren's remains would

be taken out in the morning. "I am going in the plane," added Edna.

"No," Victoria said, aware that her friend hated flying more than anything. "Don't you do that," implored Victoria. "It isn't necessary."

"I am going in the plane," said Edna.

Victoria knew better than to insist; Edna's configuration of planets gave her a surprisingly stubborn character in some situations.

"Vicky," said Edna, "a detective came to see me today. He asked questions about Warren."

"Why did he get in touch with you?"

"Because I made the—arrangements."

"Well, that's routine."

"I think it means the authorities aren't done with the case."

"Huh," scoffed Victoria. "They see a few people to make the report look good."

"Are they really that cynical, Vicky?"

Victoria thought of movies and books, of the cops who keep sleazy mistresses, who take bribes, who are swamped with so much work that they can only find time for the glamorous cases. "Edna," she said, "they think Warren was a dope fiend and if they tried to make thorough investigations of every dope fiend murdered because of drugs, they would never get anything solved." It occurred to Victoria that her own commitment to the case justified this rather injudicious appraisal of the police and their methods. She understood clearly that she was jealous of her right to defend her nephew, but that knowledge didn't deter her; if anything, it strengthened her resolve.

"No, Edna, if anybody is going to do anything for Warren, I am."

"But *what* are you doing, Vicky? I don't even know where you're calling from."

"I'm in Las Vegas."

"Las Vegas?" Her voice rose thinly in dismay.

"I'm not here to *gamble*, Edna. Don't you worry, I know what I'm doing."

After a pause Edna, loyal in spite of these mysteries, said, "I know you know what you're doing. I believe you." She added, "But will you keep me informed?"

"I will, dear friend."

After the phone call, Victoria started to read again, slipping into full absorption with the story, and so it startled her when the door flung open. Her assigned roommate entered the room, face flushed, a frown on her lips. She was a tall, slim woman in her forties, wearing a low-cut gold lamé dress. She threw her handbag on the other bed and blew out her breath wearily.

"What a night!" Her excessively red lips pouted. Eye makeup had run, giving her the look of someone with four eyes—two green and two black. "I don't think I can stick out this damn tour."

Victoria put her book down. "What happened?"

"Nothing, that's what happened. He herded us around from one spot to another like a bunch of sheep. I'm tired from just walking." She giggled. "But that one woman—I can't remember her name—she's pretty fat and wears a lot of chunky jewelry?"

It was the Pisces. "Miss Lindenbaum," said Victoria.

"Yeah, well, somehow with all that moving around, she managed to get dead drunk. What's our driver's name?"

"Mr. Carver."

"Carver had to drag her out of the Crystal Palace. It was a sight to see! Then she passed out in the bus and it took Carver and three of our old fellas to carry her back to her room."

"Poor woman," Victoria murmured, watching her roommate fling off clothing.

"What's poor about her?" the roommate exclaimed. "Some of that stuff she wears is worth money."

90

Victoria watched the woman disappear into the bathroom from which she called in a loud voice, "Mrs. Welch?"

"Call me Vicky."

"Okay, I'm Karen. Listen, did you ever go on a tour like this before?"

"This is the first time."

"For me too—and the *last*. A girl friend swore I'd meet men on a tour like this, and look at what we've got—boys of three and six, a newlywed, and a busload of geriatrics. Jesus, my makeup ran. I look like something the cat dragged in." She came back into the room, wearing panties and a bra, displaying an athletic body, kept lean and muscled by exercise and dieting. Victoria was sure of the method, because her own sister, Anne, had possessed the same kind of body, preserved by that kind of regimen. And Anne, like this woman, had also been an Aries: cocksure, aggressive, and somewhat cold.

"People told me," Karen continued from the bathroom where she'd returned with a small kit, "the best way to be a divorced lady was to take trips. But I didn't have much money, so here I am. You get what you pay for."

Victoria barely heard the words, for she was remembering her sister and her sister's husband and the phone call at midnight explaining the automobile accident that had killed them both ten years ago.

"If I had the money," Karen said, appearing in a sheer black nightgown with white cream on her face, "I'd ditch this tour tomorrow."

"I don't blame you," Victoria said, watching the woman impatiently light a cigarette and slump down on the bed. "At your age, I probably would too."

"I wouldn't mind so much, but nothing ever happens. That driver barks into the mike about scenery and a fat lady gets drunk. But I guess nothing is supposed to happen on one of these tours." She sighed. "What's funny?"

"Funny?"

"From the way you're smiling, I must have said something funny."

"No, I'm just thinking of a tour I heard of that was *quite* eventful."

Karen slipped into bed, puffed wearily on the cigarette, smashed it out, and turned off her bedside light.

Victoria immediately turned off hers.

"You don't have to do that," Karen said. "I can sleep with a light on."

"I'm ready to sleep, too."

"Well, what was so eventful about it? Someone get raped? Fat chance of that!"

"A lot of people were killed."

"Oh, an accident?"

"They were murdered," Victoria said without thinking.

"How?"

"Nobody knows."

"Well, I guess anything, even murder, would be better than *this*."

A perfect Arien response, Victoria thought. After a while she drifted into sleep on images of her family's deaths: Harry clutching his chest that fateful afternoon; Anne and Bruce in their closed caskets; and the substance of Warren blown into the air currents above the Pacific. But her last waking memory was of Mr. Carver's remark about the recent accident: one in a million. . . .

The next morning while Mr. Carver was storing luggage in the rear compartment, Victoria took her usual seat and noticed among the other passengers approaching the bus a man she had never seen before, carrying a suitcase. Before departure he entered the bus with Mr. Carver, who motioned toward the aisle. The new passenger stood at the front and gazed down the rows. He was a tall, impeccably dressed man in his fifties, with thinning brown hair and a sharply featured face. Across the aisle the divorcee Karen began to glow with anticipation and in an unconscious gesture her hand rose to her hair.

Victoria was also expectant in Karen's behalf and so she was surprised and even disappointed when the new arrival moved slowly down the aisle and without one glance at Karen, who was smiling fiercely up at him, asked if the seat next to Victoria was taken and then sat down where yesterday the fat Pisces had snored.

For the second time in a week Alexander Boyle had flown down to San Diego. He had no trouble finding Edna Sutton's address, and in a rented car drove out to her small house in the Hillcrest district. To the pale, stately woman he introduced himself as a police detective and flashed a badge, which she waved away with an embarrassed flutter of her hand. Edna Sutton ushered him into a neat, sparsely furnished parlor, kept in semi-darkness with closed shades and two lamps weakly burning, although outside the sun was still bright. He was struck by the number of framed drawings on the walls. A quick appraisal suggested that they were all by the same artist, and he was peering at them when the tall woman asked him would he care for tea.

"Thank you, no." He sat on the overstuffed sofa she indicated, while for herself she took a straight-backed cane chair. He told her that he was investigating the death of Warren Shore; because she had made the funeral arrangements, he had come to her for information.

Edna Sutton claimed to know very little about the boy, who was the nephew of a friend.

Boyle studied the woman, whose thin and high-cheeked face gave the impression of inner strength but also of a rather dreamy character, as if her energies were concentrated on problems most people overlook or avoid. He could probably believe what she said, but she would probably say little if he were clumsy.

93

Gently he asked if it were possible for him to see the dead boy's aunt.

That seemed to fluster the woman, so quickly he added, "I assure you, I'll try not to upset her."

"Oh, I believe that. Only I'm afraid she's not available." Then she explained that Miss Welch had taken a bus tour.

"A bus tour?"

"I know that sounds unfeeling at a time like this," the woman said in a thin voice, "but she considered the trip necessary."

"I see," Boyle replied warily and glanced up at a bank of drawings on the wall in front of him. "By the way, I'm impressed by those."

"You are?" The woman began to smile.

"Yes, art's my hobby."

"That's quite unusual for a policeman, isn't it?"

"I'm told it is. Really, I like them. They're all by the same artist?"

Her smile broadened. "Yes, they are."

"I like the line—economical, but it gives the illusion of deep space. And there's a dreamlike quality to the forms. They remind me a little of Miró, but with their own presence."

"Thank you."

"Then they're yours?"

"Yes." She avoided his eyes, but smiled to indicate the depth of her pride. Like most artists, she was the easy prey of flattery.

"Do you show?" he asked, pressing the advantage.

"Oh, never."

"But you should."

"You think so?"

"In my opinion, you should." And actually he meant it; the work had unmistakable authority and élan. But he wasn't here to discover an artist, so he asked abruptly for the name of the bus tour that Shore's aunt had taken.

Still buoyed by the discussion of her drawings, Edna Sutton told him immediately. Then surprise at his request seemed to overtake her. "Is that important?" she asked.

"Well, it could be. In our investigation we may want some information from her quickly. If we know where the bus is, we can contact her right away."

"Oh, of course. Wouldn't you like some tea now?"

Boyle got up to leave. "I'm sorry but I must go." He looked at the drawings again, then led the way to the door. There he turned and once again caught her off guard.

"You said her trip was necessary?"

"She told me it was. You see, she feels a bus trip of some sort is connected with her nephew's death."

"That's an interesting idea. Do you agree?"

Edna Sutton shrugged, a dreamy expression settling over her eyes again, now the subject was no longer art. "I don't know anything about it."

He believed her.

"But Vicky will do what she thinks right," the woman added. "How she loved that boy."

The bus was heading north from Las Vegas into the desert. Through the tinted glass of the windows the passengers watched sagebrush blowing and grouse clicking over the hard earth. Victoria was already chatting pleasantly with the new man, although over his shoulder she often caught Karen glaring at them. Mr. Boyle had decided to join the tour after a few disappointing days at the dice tables of Las Vegas. He was a polite man, asking her permission to smoke, although it was hard for her to guess what he was thinking. His face was impassive, either from intent or natural composure. His steady gray eyes seemed kind enough, and yet at certain moments they narrowed in a way that chilled her. She decided that the man was fascinating, but then secretive people had always attracted her. She decided to guess his sign.

95

"Don't tell me the month you were born in," she said. "Let me guess it. First of all, what sort of activities do you like?"

Mr. Boyle laughed. "Eating."

"Ah hah!"

"Is that important?"

"Very. Go on."

"Well, I like art. In fact, I'm a dealer."

"How are you with money?"

"I suppose fairly close."

"Do possessions mean much to you?"

"I'm afraid so. I'm a born collector."

"What about love?" In response to his arch look—actually his first definite expression—she added, "I'm serious. Do you consider yourself sensual?"

"I do." He paused thoughtfully. "Yes, I do."

"I don't mean only sex. I mean are you moved more by beauty than by ideas?"

"Definitely."

"Are you loyal?"

"Exceptionally so, I've been told."

"Is your health good?"

"Well, it has been. But I'm supposed to be on a strict diet."

"Do you keep on it?"

Mr. Boyle shook his head.

"Then you consider yourself a bit self-indulgent?"

"More than a bit, I'm afraid." His eyes suddenly narrowed in the way that chilled and fascinated her. "Are these questions getting you anywhere?"

"I think so. I'm almost ready to guess. Are you especially fond of family life?"

"I was."

Victoria sighed emphatically. "One more question. Do you love music?"

"Next to art it's my passion."

"Were you born in May?"

96

She was delighted to see his face twist into a puzzled frown.

"How did you know that?"

"You have all the traits of a Taurus." Then she added almost without thinking, "Except for your special kind of intensity. The Taurean is usually more relaxed. But that could be due to your ascendant or your moon."

"What are they?"

"I'm afraid I couldn't tell you without making a chart, and I didn't bring my materials. What date in May?"

"The third."

"Now that's interesting! You were born on the same day as Niccolò Machiavelli."

They both laughed, but Victoria could see that his eyes were cheerless and it was now clear to her that there was something distressing about this man, something that both challenged and repelled her. It was not that, like most people, he had taken a supercilious view of her belief in astrology. The unsettling effect he had upon her was the result of an unfathomable personality. Although much about him was Taurean and pleasant, within this man was also a life of secrets, probably ruled over by Saturn and Mars, by darkness and violence, and through this world of shadows he marched in full authority. How fitting it was that for such a journey she had found such a companion!

But they were laughing about his kinship with Machiavelli, and the amiable sound of it had Karen glowering at them disconsolately.

Near the dry, dusty little town of Panaca, the bus stopped and the passengers got out for a look at Cathedral Gorge, a vast chasm eroded by wind, spectacularly colored, with rising spires and arches. Boyle stayed close to the plump little woman whose trail he had been following ever since leaving Miss Sackman's office. Notwithstanding the mumbo jumbo about astrology, Victoria Welch was obviously no fool. Her tiny blue eyes seemed to miss nothing as he strolled with her through the clear, hot morning toward a vantage point from which to view the gorge. She made a strange, somewhat humorous investigator in her rumpled skirt and flowered blouse, but according to her friend, Edna Sutton, that was precisely what she meant to be, an investigator. She had actually taken this trip to find her nephew's murderer! Of course, her chance of doing that was mathematically hopeless, and yet her method was the right one. Evidently her nephew had told her of the robbery and therefore she *knew* that people on a similar tour had died in a bus long before they were found dead in an accident. Sooner or later Boyle might have to eliminate a person with such information. If, however, he did so before discovering the goods, he would defeat his purpose. Never before had he been in a comparable situation. Possibly the only person who could help him recover the goods had unwittingly set out to prove him a murderer.

Everyone was hot and thirsty after returning from the gorge, and even when Mr. Carver turned on the air conditioner, there was grumbling throughout the bus. He announced over the mike that since it was nearly a hundred miles through barren country before they reached the Lehman Caves, they would stop midway at a federal agricultural station for refreshments and a rest. A cheer went up.

Karen took this opportunity to question Boyle.

"The agricultural station isn't listed in the tour brochure, is it?"

Boyle shrugged, attempting to hide his astonishment at what the driver had just announced. "I really don't know."

"But will the government allow us on the station?" she persisted, smiling a smile that had nothing to do with her question.

"I wouldn't think so," Boyle replied hesitantly. "I would guess they'd turn us away."

"That's my guess, too."

98

"Excuse me," Victoria Welch said and left her seat.

Boyle watched curiously as she swayed down the aisle and leaned over the driver's shoulder.

"But on the other hand," said Karen animatedly, "the tour might have made some sort of arrangement. I don't think we've formally met. I am Karen Hill."

Boyle introduced himself without enthusiasm, watching the librarian up front. The woman opposite him was saying something more when Victoria returned and halted at their row.

"I found out," Victoria said to Karen.

"Oh, you did," Karen replied listlessly, her face expectant and brightly turned toward Boyle.

He got up and let the librarian take her seat by the window.

"Mr. Carver says the custodian will let us on the station because it's Sunday. It's not official, but it's done."

"Really?" Boyle said.

"Mr. Carver called this morning from Vegas. The custodian'll have sandwiches and everything ready."

"I hope he has the martinis ready," put in Karen, with a wink at Boyle.

He hunched down in his seat and closed his eyes, pretending to sleep. Later he opened them to meet Victoria Welch's inquiring stare.

"Anything wrong?" she asked quietly.

"Wrong? Why, no. What could be wrong?"

"I just got the feeling—" She gestured a little with both hands. "Well, I couldn't say."

"I'm just thirsty," he explained, forcing a smile.

"Ah, your Taurean nature!"

But something really was wrong, and now it was too late for Alexander Boyle to do a thing about it. Forlornly he asked the air how was it that people could make the same mistake again and again and again.

6

Few animals stirred under the blazing Nevada sun. A goat shuffled along the wire fence, a couple of chickens pecked at the dry earth of their pen, some cows slapped tails against their flanks, but otherwise the station was motionless under the noonday heat. Balers, rotary hoes, and grain combines stood behind the clump of white buildings like prehistoric beasts poised to spring, their hard plating crusted with dirt. Beyond the station a herd of grazing sheep on an experimental range lifted their black faces in unison at the sound of a motor. Soon the bus appeared over the horizon, surging through whirls of dust on the flat, straight macadam. Before the bus entered the open main gate and swung into the parking lot, a thin old man in overalls and wide-brimmed cowboy hat was already waiting outside the largest building. He stood there grinning while the disembarking passengers moved sluggishly into the heat, their eyes squinting from the brightness of the sun. Mr. Carver came out last, accompanied by Victoria Welch and Alexander Boyle.

"How ya doing, Henry?" said the old man extending his hand to Mr. Carver.

"Good, and you, Ben?"

"I'm just fine, considering." The custodian glanced at the passengers in small groups strolling around the lot, peering idly at the buildings and beyond at the livestock stalls. "We been having some goings-on here."

"Yeah, well, I've got some bad news for you. Paul Reskin had an accident."

The old custodian raised his bushy eyebrows. "That so?"

"Went over a cliff with a whole busload."

"On the last trip he come through here?"

"That's right." The two men started to walk toward the largest building, with Boyle and Victoria Welch and then others following them.

"It certainly is hot," Victoria commented and Boyle nodded silently.

The two men led the passengers into the building, which seemed especially cool and dark in contrast to the heat and brightness outside. They went down a long corridor lined on either side by offices for hydrophonics, land reclamation, entomology, soil testing. At the end of the corridor was a cafeteria with cheese, jelly, and ham sandwiches stacked behind the counter. Mr. Carver helped the custodian pass them out along with Cokes, cups of iced tea, and coffee. At the end of the line, Victoria Welch asked Boyle if she could get him a glass of water.

"No, thanks," he said.

"I thought you were thirsty."

"Not for water."

They sat down together at a table and watched latecomers, who had stopped at the rest rooms, move with trays along the line. The room filled with the gentle hum of voices. Karen, one of the last to get her snack, searched the tables and came over to the one occupied by Boyle and the librarian. "Is all this free?" she asked gaily.

"The old man will collect later," Boyle said.

"Yes, and charge us *double*." Karen sat down without a

101

word for Victoria. "But what the hell," she said to Boyle, "it's worth it, isn't it? That desert's terrible even when you're inside the bus. What do you have there?" She pointed to the pile of sandwiches on Boyle's tray.

"Cheese," he said, watching Victoria Welch abruptly rise. "Ham—" He followed her progress among the tables across the room to where the custodian and Mr. Carver sat.

"Jelly—"

"You're one of those lucky people who don't have to watch their weight," Karen chattered. "Me, if I ate like that I'd weigh a *ton*. But men have an easier time of it. Why, my ex could—"

"Excuse me a moment," Boyle said, rising. Swiftly he left the cafeteria and hurried to the public phone booth he had seen in the corridor. He put a dime in and placed a collect call to San Francisco. A girl told the operator that Mr. Hirschorn was away from his desk at the moment.

"Locate him," broke in Boyle. "This is urgent."

The operator agreed to try again in five minutes. Boyle paced back and forth in front of the booth, smelling on the cool air a mixture of disinfectant and livestock fodder. Across the hall from the booth an office door, labeled CROP ANALYSIS, was slightly ajar, so he went in there and sat down at a desk, having from the window a clear view of the station's water tank, a squat, gunmetal gray cylinder gleaming in the sunlight. A sour smile twisted Boyle's mouth as he looked at the tank and waited and waited. When the phone rang, he leaped to his feet and rushed across the hall to the booth.

Hirschorn's voice immediately assumed the formal tone of the realtor.

"Send your secretary out of the room," Boyle urged. "I can't wait for another call." He heard the realtor say, "Xerox ten copies of the Weingott prospectus, Janette." Then: "That'll keep her busy, Alex, but I don't like talking here."

"I'm at the agriculture station outside of Baker."

"What?" Hirschorn shouted, then in a lower voice said, "What in hell are you doing *there*?"

"I can't explain now. But they're letting tourists on the station."

"That's hard to believe."

"But that's what they're doing."

"Must be some mix-up—"

"A goddamn custodian is letting them on the station."

"I thought that custodian—"

"This is *another* one," Boyle interrupted angrily. "Nobody bothered to stop *him*." He turned to see if anyone was coming down the corridor.

"Maybe they thought it would be better to go along as before. Nothing can happen now, anyway."

"Yes, but something *is* happening." He saw the newlyweds strolling hand in hand down the hall toward him. "Listen, I'll call you later. Tonight."

Boyle hung up the phone, smiled tightly at the passing couple, and hurried back to the cafeteria, where Carver and the custodian were passing among the tables, collecting for the snacks.

Boyle scanned the room, meeting the uplifted smiling face of Karen Hill. But Victoria Welch was nowhere in sight.

A few minutes earlier, when she had left Mr. Boyle and Karen for the custodian's table, Victoria had been trembling with anticipation. This must be the way detectives felt when accidentally they overheard the chance word, the unguarded phrase, the innocent remark that opens up to them a whole new network of thought. She had overheard the custodian speak of "goings-on," and from that instant she had scarcely been able to conceal her excitement. Throughout the trip she had looked in vain for a sign of recent disruption of routine, either in the bus or on the route, and perhaps (this was her own wry conclusion) only her amateurish enthusiasm had kept her from despairing. Now, as

103

she crossed the room toward the custodian and bus driver, she felt herself on the verge of discovery—it was a familiar feeling, one that she had during library research when she was tracking down a difficult piece of information for a reader, the thrilling intuition that this catalogue or this reference book would unearth the fact.

"May I sit down?" she asked the two men pleasantly.

"Ain't every day a handsome lady wants to sit with this old man," the custodian said gallantly and got up to help her with the chair.

"I'm tired of the same old talk over there," Victoria said, nodding toward the tourist tables. "I couldn't help overhearing you say you'd had some goings-on here lately. Something interesting?"

"I don't know how interesting you'd call it, lady, but I was just telling Henry here we lost some people this week."

"Lost them?"

"Yeah, a bunch was transferred out. Here one day, gone the next." He turned to Henry Carver. "Fred was one of 'em."

"No kidding," said Mr. Carver, who explained to Victoria that Fred was the other custodian.

"Yep, here one day, gone the next," said the custodian, chomping his gums, a stain of chewing tobacco at the edge of his mouth. "Transferred 'em without no notice, I understand." He shook his head gloomily. "It ain't no way to treat folks."

"It certainly isn't," Victoria agreed. "What did they do to be transferred?"

"That's the point I was making. Didn't do nothing, I understand. They was just pulled out."

"Their families, too?"

The old man shrugged. "Nobody tells me nothing around here." He turned to Carver. "This was a good place to work, Henry, till they brung in all them new people."

Mr. Carver nodded judiciously, swinging his blunt little

104

hand through the air for emphasis. "It's the same every-where. Nothing makes sense anymore."

"I'm a librarian," Victoria told them, forgetting her new role for a moment and remembering old Sackman. "Last year they brought in a new chief librarian with political connections. Did it over everybody's head."

"That's it," sighed the custodian. "Them new people from the East don't know a sheep from a goat, but they think they own the place."

"Veterinarians who don't know a sheep from a goat?" laughed Victoria.

"It's the damn truth, lady, to hear the old vets tell it." He turned to Carver. "Them labs," he pointed across the cafe-teria at a door marked LABORATORIES NO ADMISSION, "was al-ways kinda pleasant. You went in and out and got a good morning from the vets. Way it is now, nobody says nothing. I go through there without a fare-thee-well from any of them new fellas."

Mr. Carver grunted, wagging his head savagely. "The same everywhere. Nothing's like it used to be."

"Do the veterinarians live on the station?" Victoria asked.

"Most of 'em live in Ely," said the custodian. "I was talking to Doctor Arms yesterday—" He looked at Victoria. "One of the old-timers here. A big, good-looking fella. The *ladies* sure think so." He turned and gave Mr. Carver a masculine wink, which was not lost on Victoria, who all her life had bristled to see men wink at men in wordless admiration of the sexual prowess of other men.

"He used to gab with me," said the custodian, "just like folks, but yesterday I kidded him a little and he says, 'Ben, you're bothering me. You're bothering me,' he says."

"Nothing's like it was," agreed Mr. Carver with a sigh.

Victoria stared at them a moment, then excused herself, and ambled toward the laboratory door across the room. Waiting until the two men's attention was turned, she tried the door and quickly opened it. Then she was in a corridor similar to the one they had all entered after leaving the bus, with offices along the way. Most of these were unlabeled, however. On impulse and after a guilty backward glance, she tried one of the office doors, but it was locked. Again she glanced back, then tried another and found this one open. Slowly she swung the door wide and stuck her head inside the room. It smelled medicinal and at the same time pungent with the animal odor of a pet shop. Along the walls were cages filled with mice, chickens, and dogs, and benches equipped with sinks and scientific tubing and beakers of the kind she had shuddered to see on anti-vivisectionist posters. A caged dog began to bark at her, so quickly she shut the door and moved rapidly down the corridor until coming to an exit. The next moment she was standing in blazing white sunlight, squinting at a penful of grunting hogs.

"Hello there," Boyle called to her as they prepared to board the bus. "I missed you in the cafeteria."

"Yes, I took a walk. Oh—" She opened her large handbag, fumbling through Kleenex and things that rattled. "Did you pay for my snack?"

Boyle put a restraining hand on her arm, smiling as pleasantly as he could, seeing in her sunglasses his own reflected image—distorted and wavering. Just then two small boys swirled around his legs in a game of tag, their distracted mother clutching at them, and when he looked up he saw that Victoria Welch had walked over to the old custodian. He watched the two of them part familiarly with a handshake and then Victoria Welch board the bus with her cheeks flushed, her mouth faintly parted.

Soon the bus was heading north again. Creosote bushes and desert scrub gave way to bunch grass for grazing, the range was dotted with cattle and sheep herds, and the mountains moved closer in the landscape. In another hour they were at the Lehman Caves, exploring the cool passageways of caverns bristling with stalactites and stalagmites, among which the bones of Indian dead had lain for centuries. Boyle watched the plump librarian amble along the dimly lit path, her face tilted toward each interesting sight, her broad back hunched in concentration, as if there were nothing on her mind but the task of absorbing, like any good tourist, the sights she was paying to see. Yet she had acted strangely at the station. What had she wanted to learn from the old custodian? What had roused her curiosity?

After an hour's tour, the bus reloaded and went through Connor's Pass, entering cooler air. From the high mountains surrounding them juniper, piñon, and stunted mahogany thrust into the clear sky, and by the time they reached Ely at sunset Mr. Carver had turned off the air conditioner. Rooms were booked for them at a hotel which had a bar and casino. Boyle saw to it that he ate with Victoria Welch, but unfortunately that nuisance of a divorcee came along, too. Boyle ate and drank too much, sullenly wondering what to do about the librarian. If only she drank—that would loosen her tongue—but she merely sipped tea, and then to his disappointment, she pleaded fatigue and went up to bed, leaving him at the table with Karen Hill, who snatched at his sleeve and begged him to take her into the casino, because a lady couldn't go alone. With a smile, steeling himself for an unpleasant hour or two with the gay divorcee, Alexander Boyle opened his wallet to buy chips.

Victoria ran her forefinger down half a column of names in the Ely phone book before coming to Arms, DVM. She took a deep breath and picked up the phone.

The masculine voice which answered was gruff and impatient.

"This is Doctor Arms. Who's calling?"

"My name is Welch, I'm on a bus tour, and I'd very much like to talk to you."

"About what?"

"I'd prefer to tell you in person."

"A bus tour?" She heard him grunt. Was he laughing at her or angry or incredulous?

"I'm on a bus tour and that's what I want to see you about."

"Are you selling something?"

"Doctor, this is important. I'd appreciate only a few minutes of your time. I'm certainly not selling anything."

"Call me at the Baker Agricultural Station tomorrow."

"That's the problem. You see, the bus leaves in the morning. It must be tonight."

There was a long pause, then Victoria heard another voice in the background, and Dr. Arms' half-whispered, impatient answer, "I'm telling you I don't know."

"It really is important," Victoria persisted.

"Well. Could you make it right away?"

"Immediately. I have your address, I can take a cab."

"Then, if it's *really* important," he said without hiding his exasperation.

A couple of minutes later, hurrying through the hotel lobby, Victoria caught a glimpse of Mr. Boyle's broad back next to Karen's narrow one, both bent over the emerald green of a casino table. It was a short ride by taxi to the small frame house on a treeless street. A tall, husky man in boots, jeans, and plaid shirt opened the door for her. From the sudden relaxation of his questioning face, Victoria understood that her appearance was a relief to him. She remembered the custodian's wink and wondered if Dr. Arms had expected a pretty girl who could cause him trouble. That possibility was strengthened when Victoria followed him into the house and saw a woman's curious face moving past an open door into a farther room. The big man ushered her into a den which was dominated by a huge glassed-in guncase. Antlered deer and trout stared down from the walls. There was a definite smell of leather, hay, and cigar smoke commingling in the air. Victoria sat on the edge of the overstuffed chair the veterinarian pointed to.

108

"Okay, now what is it?" he said curtly, sitting opposite her. One look at the way he crossed his legs and set his handsome but sullen face was enough to warn Victoria that he intended to be difficult.

She decided on a bold approach. "Doctor, a relative of mine was killed recently in a bus accident. He was on a tour that stopped at your agricultural station."

The man shook his head, his lips tight in denial. "We don't allow visitors on the station."

"His bus stopped there last Sunday for refreshments, just like our bus stopped there today."

Dr. Arms dismissed her assertion with a little wave of his big hand. Now that she no longer threatened him—what had he expected, the outraged sister of a girl he'd seduced?— this broad-shouldered John Wayne of a man was going to treat her doubtlessly as he treated most women, including the shadowy wife who moved anxiously through the background of his life: with disdain.

But Victoria clung to her bold approach. "I'm convinced the bus accident was the *direct* result of something that happened along the route."

"What's your point, Miss Welch?" he asked.

She stared at the shoe of his crossed leg; that shoe was huge enough to hold two pounds of loose tea. From his cold restraint, his impatience with anything but facts, she guessed he was a Virgo, possibly with Aries rising, but she suppressed the desire to ask and instead explained with the kind of Virgeon coolness that he would admire, how the bus had plunged over a California cliff (she did not mention Warren or the robbery) under peculiar circumstances, which caused her to suspect that a chain of events leading back through the tour had resulted in the accident.

"You're not making sense to me," Dr. Arms said when she paused. He recrossed his legs, reminding Victoria of two great logs slowly tumbling over each other in a lumber jam she had once seen on an Oregon river during a backpacking trip years ago with her beloved husband.

This flashing memory of her husband leaped to one of Warren lugging that laundry bag of stolen property into her apartment, and her resolve stiffened, her voice rose into a spiky tone of demand. "Doctor," she said, "exactly *what* happened on the station last week?" When his face tensed into a scowl, she added, "Is it true a number of people were transferred?"

"What is this, a cross-examination?" he scoffed, grabbing a cigar from a humidor next to his chair.

"Is it true, Doctor?"

"Sure it's true." He lit the cigar with the strong flame of a butane lighter and snapped it shut angrily.

"Were any of them *new* people?"

"New people?"

"I understand there's been a new group of veterinarians on the station."

"I don't know where you get your information, but it's all wrong. There hasn't been a new employee on the station in a year. Now I'm sorry, but this isn't getting us anywhere." He put his beefy hands on the chair arms, preparing to rise.

"Then they *all* came about a year ago?" she persisted and for an answer, he got swiftly to his feet and glared down at her.

Rising too, Victoria brushed the wrinkles from her skirt and watched him cross the room to the door. "Doctor," she said.

He turned and squinted through cigar smoke.

"This is the point," she said, returning his stare. "I think something happened on the station that led to them being transferred. *And* at the time the bus passed through."

For a reply the veterinarian opened the study door and gestured for her to leave.

But she held her ground. "Doctor," she said, "were those new people veterinarians?"

"The Department of Agriculture is none of your business, lady. Now I've been patient—" He raised his shoulders; it was an almost imperceptible movement, but a singularly menacing one, and so Victoria reluctantly followed him out of the room into the hall. In the foyer Victoria turned toward him, seeing past his left arm a thin woman scramble across the hall into the study to wait hopefully for an explanation she wouldn't believe.

"Doctor," Victoria said, looking squarely into his frowning face, "do those new people know a sheep from a goat?"

The man swung the front door wide. "What gives you the right," he hissed, "to come here at ten o'clock at night and ask a lot of stupid questions? The Department of Agriculture is none of your business."

"But it is!" Victoria declared, her anger replacing uneasiness. "I am a citizen!"

"Then dammit, write your Congressman," he muttered as she swept past him into the cool night air.

Victoria walked rapidly down the street, gripping the collar of her raincoat as the full chill of the Nevada evening swept through her. During a cold mile's walk back to the hotel, Victoria mumbled bitterly, "That man, that *man!*" His crude treatment of her had shaken her confidence. Had her questions really been stupid? Certainly she had grasped wildly at any surmise that came into her head. But one thing was sure: Dr. Arms had been more evasive than her questions warranted. He had reacted like a man fearful of making important disclosures, and that meant at least *some* of her questions had hit the mark. Something indeed had happened out there among the penned hogs and caged mice.

She was still absorbing the full impact of the interview when she opened the door of her room and saw Karen Hill sitting up in bed, cream on her face, a movie magazine lying across her black-gowned stomach.

"Where have you been?" Karen asked.

"I took a walk."

111

"In this weather?" Karen shook her head and sighed. "First we sweat, then we shiver. I'd ditch this tour if I had the money."

"Did you lose at roulette?" Victoria asked with a smile.

"I won five bucks, but I had a damn dull time of it, thank you."

Victoria picked up her pajamas and went into the bathroom to change. She called from there, "Didn't you like Mr. Boyle?"

"Huh."

Victoria changed and with a tissue rubbed off the little bit of lipstick she wore, then brushed her teeth, and returned to the room.

"I thought you liked him," she said.

"He's a nothing."

"Well, he seems pleasant enough."

"To you. To *you* he *is*. I honestly believe he's interested in you."

Victoria laughed.

"I'm not kidding. The whole time I was with him, which wasn't long, he was always talking about *you*. Weren't *you* nice and what did I think of *you* and had we made friends."

Again Victoria laughed.

"I mean it. Only two things wake him up: food and *you*."

Victoria sat on the edge of the bed, thoughtfully considering what Karen had said. "I guess I should be flattered."

"I guess you should be. I guess *I* would be, but only because he's the one eligible male on the whole damn tour." Karen snorted and lit a cigarette. "Never again! Before I waste money on a tour again, I'll join the YWCA or go back to my ex."

Victoria slipped into bed and turned toward the wall.

"Mind if I keep the light on awhile?" Karen asked.

"Not at all."

"I'm nervous, I can't sleep," Karen fretted. "I tried all day with that joker and never even got a smile. I have a strange

112

feeling about him. Did you notice he never says anything about himself?" Karen sat bolt upright and puffed vigorously on the cigarette. "How come a man like that shows up on the kind of stupid tour we're on? You know, he could be running. Somebody could be after that man. He could even be a jailbird. I mean, he eats like he'd been starved." Karen's eyes were shining. "People say I jump to conclusions, and my ex was always telling me the worst thing about me was my imagination. But I don't care. I have strong intuitions about people. Believe me, this man is running away." Karen blinked rapidly in response to the boldness of her own ideas. Then nervously she puffed and put out the cigarette with a fierce twist. "Anyway, tomorrow he is going to get the cold shoulder. I'm proud. I'm not at the point *yet* I have to chase men. Tomorrow he won't even get a hello from me!"

Victoria didn't hear this declaration, having fallen asleep almost at the moment her exhausted body touched the bed.

Having disposed of a rasher of bacon and three fried eggs —the worst possible breakfast for someone with a high cholesterol count—Alexander Boyle walked into the lobby. He was going to the news counter, when he saw Victoria Welch huddled in animated conversation with a little bellhop. Boyle got a magazine and turned to meet the librarian's passing smile. "You're a late riser!" he called brightly and received from her a coy flick of the hand.

When she had disappeared into the coffee shop, Boyle walked straight over to the old bellhop, who was sitting on a bench by the window, his faded blue uniform hanging on him with a voluminous looseness that reminded Boyle suddenly of Warren Shore in his oversized coat.

Boyle said, "I noticed that lady talking to you."

"Yeah?" The bellhop looked up quizzically from a face leather-brown and tight to a small skull.

"I'd like to know what she asked," Boyle said.

"Yeah?"

Boyle opened his wallet and shoved an FBI identification card in the bellhop's face, which changed expression quickly from defiant amusement to respect.

"Yes, sir."

"Now, what about the lady?"

The bellhop uncrossed his legs and sat up straight. "Yes, sir. She wanted to know about that rumor."

"What rumor?"

"Well, there's been talk about them people from the ag station."

"Go on."

"It ain't no more'n talk, sir. It's jist that eight, ten of 'em living here left town all at once. You and me know how folks are. Eight, ten people leave town suddenly, there's gonna be talk." He pursed his lips over nearly toothless gums. "That's what I told that lady. It's talk. There's nothing in it."

"That's not for you to decide," Boyle replied severely.

"Yes, sir."

"What exactly do people say?"

"I heard some of 'em say about them scientists down there, they ab—ab—took funds from the station, a real fortune, and run off."

"Then what did the lady say?"

"She didn't say nothing, sir. I swear—" Without asking, the bellhop raised his hand to be sworn in.

"All right," Boyle said. "You understand this is government business?"

"Yes, sir, I do."

"Put your hand down," Boyle demanded.

"Yes, sir."

"You don't have to swear anything. All you have to do is keep your mouth shut about our conversation."

"Yes, sir, I know that."

"Or take the consequences."

The bellhop jumped to his feet, his mouth working nervously. "Yes, sir. You can count on me, I won't say nothing. I been in and out of the hotel business these twenty years thereabouts and I learnt how to—"

Boyle nodded glumly and turned, with that high-pitched voice trailing him, "keep my trap shut, I been doing jist that for a long, long—"

Boyle glanced into the coffee shop, seeing her hunched over coffee at the counter. Then he went to the elevator, thinking.

When they were seated on the bus, Victoria Welch was unusually animated and talkative. She kept saying what a beautiful little town Ely was, with the mountains rising above it and its quaint streets and the atmosphere of an old Western mining town. Then she couldn't find her sunglasses and kept up a running chatter, while poking around in the maw of her large handbag, extracting in her search a number of articles, among them a rabbit's foot on a chain and a police whistle. Boyle was startled by the contrast between this aging librarian with her superstitions and Victoria Welch whose dogged persistence reminded him of a professional. He watched her fleshy hand plummet again and again into the cavernous handbag, coming out finally with the sunglasses which, when set on her large nose below gray hair and a small pillbox red hat, helped to convey the image of a lonely widow touring on meager funds. As the bus drove out of town, she continued her monologue, as if words, any words, would hide feelings that should be hidden. So much talk was uncharacteristic of her. Was she exuberant or nervous? Boyle wondered.

"What was I saying?" She took a deep breath and gave him a quick, sidelong glance.

"You were telling me about your job."

"Of course. Until this year I wouldn't have traded my job with anyone, but now I'm not sure. The trouble's my boss. She's an unevolved Cancer, meaning she has all the *worst* and none of the best traits of her sign. She got the job because her brother-in-law's a wealthy man, a trustee who gave the library a large donation last year. What doubly frustrates me, though, is her ability. For one thing, she has a first-rate memory. For another, she has a fantastic sense of order. You should see her desk—never a scrap of paper on it. What she lacks, of course, is a feeling for books and people. And yet she's more effective than any of us dreamed."

"It *is* strange, isn't it," agreed Boyle. "I had an assistant in the gallery once who was just like your boss, a nonstop talker and apparently a fool, but he did a fine job, sold more paintings than I did. I was sorry to see him go, in spite of the fact I couldn't stand him."

Delivered of these chatty remarks, Boyle savored the memory of that assistant and then of the last peaceful year during which his entire energy had gone into the gallery—where it belonged. What in the hell was he doing on this bus, tailing a librarian who had become his adversary in the trickiest job of his *other* career, a career he had promised his dying wife to give up forever? He glanced at the librarian, surprised to catch her staring at him. For only a moment their eyes met unfathomably behind sunglasses, but it was long enough for Boyle to have the peculiar sensation of looking at someone who was looking at *him* for the first time.

She wrenched her gaze away from him, trying with a helpless feeling of failure to hide her astonishment. What had the man just said? "I had an assistant once who was just like your boss, *a nonstop talker*." Had she told him anything about old Sackman's garrulity? No! It wouldn't have occurred to her. After all, her own sister had talked as much, and during the years so had many of her friends. It was her frustration over Sackman's petty character, *not* Sackman's nonstop talking, that she had explained, and yet this Mr. Boyle had reacted precisely to what she *hadn't* said! Did he know Sackman, and if so, why? Victoria had no faith what-

116

soever in coincidence, the stars were strict in their course, and the reticulation of human destiny was woven by God's mathematical calculations with a precision that precluded such foolishness as coincidence. Coincidence had nothing to do with Mr. Boyle's knowledge of old Sackman. He had *sought out* the chief librarian. But for what reason? There could be only one: Sackman led to the aunt of Warren Shore!

Victoria could feel this revelation surge through her body, her face flushed and her hands trembled fisted in her lap. Would he see how agitated she was? She nailed her attention to the landscape passing by, and when the bus stopped outside of Ely for a quick tour of the Kennecott copper mine, she fussed with her handbag and waited until Boyle got up and moved down the aisle before she too rose and filed out.

She tried not to think of what she now knew: The man was following her.

The tourists stood at the rim of the mine and squinted down at the enormous pit, bister-colored in stepped layers whose wavy rings, a mile in diameter toward the edge, resembled the cross section of an enormous tree trunk. There was little enthusiasm for the windswept spectacle. People were tiring of wide horizons and cloudless sky. New acquaintances had exhausted their stores of personal history and stood apart or together but in silence. The fat, alcoholic lady leaned against the bus as if stunned, her blouse stained by sweat, her face ashen from the whiskey she had consumed last night in the casino. The old Leo woman no longer possessed the enthusiasm for dispensing little gifts of gum and candy. Boyle stood alone, watching the gay divorcee walk silently alongside Victoria Welch, who bent into the stiff breeze, both hands holding her hat down.

Something was wrong. After leaving Ely, the librarian had changed perceptibly toward him. What had happened? Boyle had been talking to her, she had been unusually animated, unusually so as if pleased and excited about something, and then abruptly she had pulled back into a cold, almost gloomy silence. Then when they reembarked, she gave him a tight little smile and took her seat next to him without a word. What could this odd withdrawal mean? Possibly it meant nothing. A common error on this sort of job, Boyle knew from experience, was to become excessively sensitive. Small doses of paranoia kept one alert, but large doses led to reckless conclusions. So he sat back and tried to calm himself by watching the mountains, grassland, and range fences float in cloudlike silence past the window, until their monotony induced a drowsiness in him and he dozed until the bus entered the border town of Wendover.

Mr. Carver announced over the speaker that they would stop for a snack before crossing into Utah. When the bus stopped and people began to rise, Boyle kept his seat. "I think I'll stay," he told Victoria with a fiercely bright smile, as she fumbled through her handbag, preparing to leave.

The look she gave him, an embarrassed confusion of forced smile and frown, confirmed his suspicion: The woman *had* changed toward him. She could hardly speak and indeed, she slipped past him into the aisle with the alacrity of someone trying to escape. He let her go, deciding not to encourage her anxiety, and while the tourists were inside the eat shop, he sat there fidgeting, increasingly convinced that something he had said or done had given him away. He was mortified by the possibility that he had unknowingly bungled like an amateur. Was he getting so old, tired, and inexpert that he couldn't even handle a librarian who kept a rabbit's foot in her bag and believed in the stars? If she was on to him, he had little chance of learning anything from her. And as for that, he had learned absolutely nothing since joining the tour. He knew now what he had known then: The strange woman was retracing the route of the bus which her nephew had robbed, and she was doing it from the outrageously heroic desire to clear the boy's name or find his killer or see justice done. Incredible. She reminded him of himself in his youth, when he had gone to war to save the world for democracy.

When the bus loaded again, she gave him another meaningless smile and then a sidelong frown and sat with her face turned resolutely toward the window. Soon they were leaving Nevada and entering a new landscape filled with shad scale, salt bush, and greasewood. Mountains to the north paralleled the road like a gigantic hedge row, while the land ahead smoothed out suddenly into an alkaline desert, shimmering glasslike in the sunlight. Mr. Carver announced over the speaker that to the left lay the Bonneville Speedway, one hundred square miles of flat salt as solid as concrete, where the fastest cars in the world were tested. The enthusiasm which had been dulled by the long journey through grassland was now renewed among passengers by this eerie trip through a white world devoid of life, the landscape of a dead planet, the aftermath of atomic holocaust. So excited was Karen Hill that she came up the aisle and exclaimed that the sight was worth the entire tour. It suddenly occurred to Boyle that these were the first words she had spoken to him all day. Had she been warned by the librarian to stay clear of him? Replying to her enthusiasm in kind, he decided that such a confidence was improbable. The librarian wouldn't confide in a woman who would ingratiate herself with any man, even if it meant betraying a trust. Boyle's eyes narrowed as he watched Karen's lithe figure return down the aisle to her seat next to the alcoholic, fat woman. Events were honing Boyle's nerves to a fine edge, and he knew it. He felt a stirring in his blood, the anticipation of action, as if thirty years had melted away and he was again a young soldier in a truck, passing through the orchards of Normandy, bound for his first battle. Since then, each time a job reached its climactic stage, he had felt the same thrill of commitment, the same dread of failure, and these mixed, heightened emotions had driven him to bouts

119

of overeating. On this job his nerves had forced him to begin the process from the outset, and by now his blood must be clogged, choking up with lazily floating globules of fat. When this job was done, he would keep to his diet and stay at home, having no more to do than prod a drunken genius like Kawabata. The barren world swept past the window, dry and icy as the moon, recalling for him the lunar landscapes of Yves Tanguy. With his adversary glumly silent beside him, Boyle let his mind wander comfortably through a gallery of images, through a mental museum in which he had stored the pleasures of a lifetime: Tobey's rhythmic temperas, Redon's dream panels, Manzu's elegant bronzes, Afro's succulent oils. At such times his other life seemed to have been lived by someone he merely knew and could not envy. Although they shared a sense of commitment, he lived in a world of peace and contemplation unknown to the other person he was.

Ahead now was the motionless silver of the Salt Lake, on either side orchards of melons and berries, and rising from the east over the glimmering stone and steel of Salt Lake City were the gullied shoulders of the Wasatch Mountains. Even when they entered the Mormon capital, he scarcely exchanged a word with the librarian, who kept her eyes fixed on the passing scene. With each passing minute she was confirming his suspicion and bringing him closer to a final determination.

The tour company had arranged for accommodations at a modest hotel near Temple Square. Boyle, who had chosen from the beginning to pay extra for a single room, went to his and placed a call to Hirschorn.

"What have you learned from the librarian?" Hirschorn asked immediately.

"Not a damn thing," said Boyle. "And you can blame that on the goddamn custodian. After talking to him, she got suspicious of me." Even as he made this claim, Boyle was disgusted by the lie. Her suspicion had been aroused *after* their departure from *Ely* and because of something he himself had done. Lies were the refuge of a fumbling, aging man who had lost his skill. In the old days Boyle would have admitted—and proudly—to an error of judgment. Now he blamed a garrulous old man for his own failure.

"Don't worry about the custodian," Hirschorn said. "The lid's been tied down on the station."

"Which is locking the barn door after the horse is gone. The incredible stupidity of those people at Baker—"

"Alex, you sound terrible. What's up?"

"I told you what's up—the woman's on to me."

"I mean what's up with *you?*"

"All right then: I'm tired, I'm disgusted, I hate this job, I never should have taken it in the first place. It looked impossible then, it *is* impossible now."

"Calm down, Alex. So you haven't learned a thing and the woman's on to you, right?"

"In a nutshell. My usefulness is finished."

"Okay, but you better stay with her until we figure out what to do."

Boyle waited, knowing that Hirschorn, good businessman that he was, was waiting for him to make the obvious decision.

"Alex?"

"Yes?"

"What do you think?"

"There's only one way to get a new lead on the goods," Boyle said reluctantly, "and that's through the woman. She carries a huge handbag and she's brought along a suitcase. Maybe something in one of them will do it."

"A slim chance, Alex."

"Have *you* got any bright ideas?"

"Not a one. Tomorrow night when the bus stops in Elko, we'll arrange for a search. Of course, we don't want you in on it. We'll bring in somebody to do it. Alex?" he added and paused. "What about her? Shouldn't we hit her?"

121

"You don't have to hit her to rob her," Boyle snapped.

"No, but you say yourself she suspects you."

"I don't like it," Boyle said gloomily, and for an instant he had a vision of the woman's nephew lying there obscenely naked with a chest wound big enough to put a fist in. "I hit my driver, I hit the kid. I'm sick of it."

"Sure you are. Only I didn't mean you should do it. The thing is, though, we've gone this far, so we better go the whole way."

Boyle knew that. Years of discipline and a lifetime of commitment overcame his aversion. "Yes, you're right," he agreed softly.

"How should it be done?"

"Well, probably at the same time her room's searched. There's a roommate, but I'll see to it she's occupied. About eleven o'clock, the librarian should be reading. She reads a lot," he added irrelevantly, recalling the times he had seen her adjust her glasses and squint down at a book in her lap, the epitome of a woman whose life has narrowed to the printed page.

"She won't make trouble before that?" asked Hirschorn.

"I don't think she knows enough yet. She's still fishing. Anyway, I can't see any way to do it earlier without getting ourselves in still more trouble."

Hirschorn laughed cheerlessly. "We don't need more. In the last two days a half dozen relatives have been demanding the property back. Funny how sharp people can be when they want something—especially the keepsakes of dead family. 'I want Johnny's watch, even if it was smashed. I gave it to him in 'fifty-nine for his birthday. Why won't you give it back to me? Are you supposed to be servants of the people? What's going on at the FBI that I can't have Johnny's watch back?'"

Boyle acknowledged the truth of this parody with a short laugh.

"And so now Hopkins is really getting nervous," Hirschorn said. "If only the bus had burned up, but it didn't."

"High tide," Boyle said ruefully. "We never thought of it hitting the rocks at high tide."

"It wasn't important then."

It had become important, Boyle admitted to himself bitterly, because he had failed to check the bus after bringing Tony Aiello the hose. Checking the bus and realizing it had been robbed would have enabled him to change the last phase of the operation. A single call to Hirschorn at that moment could have turned the trick. Burning the bus, even partially, would have made the recovery of personal effects impossible. As it was, the goods were missing without reason. Sentiment, not value would drive the next-of-kin irresistibly on: Where were those items of private worth? Did the police have them? If not, then who did? Could the bus have been robbed? How did a thief get in there if the bus was nearly submerged? Did he have a crane and blowtorches? Were steps being taken to catch him? Why hadn't the robbery been reported at the outset? Who was covering up this crime and why?

Hirschorn sighed deeply. "How long this will stay out of the news is anybody's guess now." Then clearing his throat as if settling a real estate deal, he asked Boyle, "Where will you be staying in Elko?"

"Wait." Boyle took the bus itinerary from his pocket and studied it. "At the Ranch Inn. Do you know who you'll be sending?"

"I've been thinking of Stern. He hasn't worked for a while and he's right for the job."

Stern. Boyle had worked with him once, a big hulking man who owned a lumber company in Seattle. He had three lovely daughters, one of whom was now married to a Harvard professor; and in Korea, with a special unit devoted to sabotage behind the lines, he had been an expert with the knife.

123

"Will he contact me?" Boyle asked.

"Sure. Before you go out on the town with the roommate. We'll register him as—" Hirschorn paused. "Let's say as John Hamilton."

"You're a wonder with names," Boyle laughed. "Okay then, we're set." And he added, "After this one, I'm finished."

"Sure, we both say that after every job."

"No, this is my *last*."

"I understand how you feel, Alex. You've had a bad time." In an abruptly bantering tone, an emotional shift worthy of a good businessman, Hirschorn said, "Are you following your diet?"

"What do you think?"

"I got the results yesterday of a cholesterol test and mine's high, too."

"We're getting old. Well, see you later."

"See you later. Alex? It's going to work out."

"Sure. And remember, you're buying."

Boyle didn't hang up the phone after saying good-bye, but asked the hotel operator to ring Mrs. Hill's room. Karen's initially cold response soon changed to a coquettishness that Boyle abhorred, but at least her ready acceptance of his invitation for dinner was assurance that her attitude throughout the day had resulted from his rejection of her and not from any warning given by Victoria Welch. There followed for Alexander Boyle too many cocktails, a massive steak in a restaurant converted from an old church with a waterfall in the dining room, then a succession of gloomy bars in this Mormon town, and finally a drunken kiss outside of Karen's room. It wasn't necessary for him to make love to the gay divorcee this evening—that would come tomorrow in Elko while a man by the name of Hamilton slit a librarian's throat and took her purse. When Karen opened the door and blew him a good-night kiss, Boyle had a glimpse of Victoria Welch sitting up in bed with a book propped on her lap and a frown on her face.

124

That evening after dinner in the hotel with some of the other tourists, Victoria had bought a newspaper and returned to her room. Changing for bed, she had fluffed her pillows and prepared for a few hours of reading, first the news and then Dostoevski. On the third page of the evening paper she noticed an item so astonishing that she spun out of bed and sat on its edge, bent over the print as if peering through a microscope. She read the account of a plane crash in the Bitterroot Mountains of Idaho. The pilot and nine passengers, all members of a field expedition emanating from the Federal Agricultural Station at *Baker, Nevada*, had been killed. There were no survivors.

So here it was, a fact that brought her investigation into focus. Within a single week a busload of tourists and a planeful of veterinarians had died violently, and both groups had been in proximity in the midst of the Nevada desert. This was no coincidence. It confirmed her theory of a link between the station and the bus. She could not explain why, but the destruction of two otherwise disparate groups of people had its source there, among hogs and chickens, perhaps in those new labs where mice ran in cages and dogs barked.

For a few minutes her mind raced with wild surmises: ray guns and man-killing plants, three-headed monsters and atomic radiation—the flotsam and jetsam of reading which old Sackman called trash. Even so, she was certain now that her original premise had been right: Poor Warren and the tourists had been killed for a specific reason. And now she could add to their deaths those of government employees. How she wished for her own kitchen this very moment! She liked to handle elation and despair by making a good pot of tea, preferably a zesty black. Without tea to calm her, she began pacing. She was not only elated but frightened, aware there was something to be frightened of. That station could send out tentacles.

The man who had been occupying the seat next to hers

had joined the tour solely to watch her. Of that she had proof. Perhaps he was deciding if and when *she* should die, too. After all, if maintaining secrecy had already been worth half a hundred deaths, surely one more was of no consequence. Doubtlessly she was still alive only because the man did not know the whereabouts of the stolen property. It would not keep her alive indefinitely, however, if the man and his confederates suspected her of accumulating evidence against them. She had made a serious error by failing to hide her feelings on the bus. The protagonists in mysteries would not have been so amateurish as to shrink from their pursuers, but they would have dissimulated until the last moment. That marked her for what she was: an ordinary woman, a widow, a librarian who had set out on a task beyond her abilities to handle. And yet her resolve was firmer than ever, each revelation having strengthened her aim to vindicate Warren—and now *all* the dead. She had been born on January 22, the same date as Lord Byron, and in her sign of Aquarius were men of mission and fortitude like Lincoln and Lindbergh. She was not finished yet. Victoria Welch stopped pacing, picked up the phone and called San Francisco. She had a plan.

Suffering from a hangover, Boyle emerged from the hotel and stood with other tourists awaiting Mr. Carver's signal to leave for Temple Square a few blocks away. Still tired from yesterday's exhausting trip, people straggled out into the morning sunlight. Mr. Carver grew restive and suggested that they start walking; latecomers could easily catch up. Boyle jammed on his sunglasses and fell into step behind the newlyweds. Victoria Welch hadn't come along yet, but he thought better of waiting for her, because now that her fate had been sealed, he didn't want her to become anxious from too much attention and do something impulsive. He walked slowly, however, glancing around to see if she had yet appeared. Other members of the tour came into sight,

126

and as he was mounting the hill with the granite sides of the Temple already in view and its six golden spires shimmering in the cloudless day, he caught a backward glimpse of the gay divorcee, smiling and rapidly approaching. He waited for her. For an instant he was swept by a vision of Julie Saunders climbing the hill toward him, her hair a jonquil color in the light, her face shining in anticipation of their kiss.

"Hello there," he said with fake enthusiasm.

Karen Hill was breathing hard, her skin ashen, her lips unnaturally red. "God, am I hung over. How are you?"

"The same."

"Didn't know we drank *that* much." She fell in beside him and they started to climb.

Boyle glanced over his shoulder.

"Looking for your girl friend?" Karen asked with a wry little smile.

"My girl friend?"

"Vicky Welch. Well, you won't find her. She left this morning."

Boyle halted.

"That's right. When I woke up, she was already packed. She's had it with this tour, and I don't blame her. Until last night—" Karen flashed a bright smile, "I wanted to ditch it, too. Now I'm not so sure."

"She left? Went back to San Francisco?"

"She didn't say." Karen took his arm. "Listen, I'm not all that hot for Mormon temples. Why don't we go somewhere? Hey, what's wrong?"

Boyle had clutched his chest, feeling a suffocating sensation, as if a huge rock had been suddenly placed on his rib cage. He breathed deeply a few times and then the sensation passed.

"Hey!" Karen called, as he turned without a word and started to run down the hill.

7

Twelve days prior to this frantic sprint down a hill in pursuit of a stargazing librarian who had outwitted him, Alexander Boyle had been working in his gallery on a catalogue for a new sculpture exhibition, primly anticipating a luncheon of tuna fish and salad, washed down by Tab. His assistant had gone for late morning coffee, so Boyle was alone when the call came from Hirschorn.

They hadn't spoken to each other in months, but Hirschorn's voice was airy and relaxed, meaning that he was phoning outside of his office.

After a chatty exchange of greetings, Hirschorn casually remarked that a situation had developed which might be interesting. "It's a short job, but sweet. Could you take it?"

Boyle hesitated. When Hirschorn employed a low-key sales voice, the situation was not "sweet" but messy. "I'm damn busy," Boyle told him.

"The job won't take much of your time. And I must say it's important."

"Sure, they all are."

"We need you, Alex."

Had Boyle taken a recent assignment, he still might have

refused, but it had been almost a year since he'd felt the old thrill of commitment, of challenge, of placing himself in jeopardy.

"Where do I meet you?" he said finally.

"Lobby of the Saint Franois in half an hour."

When Boyle arrived at the hotel, Hirschorn was already there and hurried across the lobby on short pudgy legs, his hand outstretched in premature greeting, his lips set in a fawning smile. But his supercilious appearance belied a tenacity which had made him both a successful realtor and a first-rate Q agent. In this man's presence Alexander Boyle felt the warmth and surety that develops among those who have shared danger.

"What's the situation?" he asked.

"Hang on to your hat." Hirschorn cracked his knuckles by intertwining his fingers and separating his palms, a habit familiar to Boyle and one that irritated him. "Some tourists drank the water on a federal agriculture station and they're all going to die." Hirschorn smiled past Boyle's shoulder and waved at a man crossing the lobby. "Hello there!" he called and turned again to Boyle. "A fella I know," he explained brightly. "Sold him a house in Forest Hill last year. Fine man but stubborn. I had to cut my commission to make the sale. You see, a mouse got out of a laboratory and poisoned the water supply."

"This happened on an *agricultural* station?" Boyle asked incredulously.

"I thought it would interest you."

It did. He understood even from this meager explanation what kind of case it was, having worked on them before. Throughout the years, in fact, he had become a specialist on cases involving potential embarrassment to the government. All of them had this in common: What initially seemed to be the blunder of a few minor officials was on further investigation the result of profound mismanagement on high levels. Another Q agent had once described such a case in terms of disease. "It's like the man who complains of a small lump in his chest—open him up and he's crawling with cancer." More than once Alexander Boyle had watched a little symptom in the boondocks lead to massive rot in Washington. A sure sign of trouble was incongruity within a system of government, and what could be more incongruous than a lethal mouse showing up on a federal agricultural station? Such toxicity had nothing to do with the welfare of cows and sheep. This didn't sound like agricultural research; this was germ warfare.

Hirschorn reached out and gently clasped Boyle's arm. "We better go up now. They're waiting for us."

"Who did the bug belong to?" Boyle asked, as they crossed the lobby toward the elevator.

"Defense."

"BW?"

Hirschorn nodded with an exasperated curl of his lips.

So Boyle knew that two departments of government were involved, a factor which emphasized the importance and difficulty of the case. Of course, it was not unheard of for agencies to cooperate on special projects or for one bureau to lend another its facilities. It was often done to juggle funds. But in Boyle's experience such collaboration was inherently dangerous and its problems far outweighed any potential benefits. He reasoned this way: On the most basic human level a man asks for trouble when he steps into another man's territory, even with permission. Compound this fundamental conflict by introducing the complexity of modern government and the stage for catastrophe is set. Authority begins to blur, communication breaks down, secrecy prevents the proper marshaling of facts, studied carelessness warps the simplest procedure, and too much or too little initiative resulting from both arrogance and envy knocks an entire project out of balance. Confusion works its way unchecked until a tiny mouse has poisoned the water supply of a hog farm and doomed a busload of innocent tourists.

"Here we are," said Hirschorn, knocking on the door of a suite on the thirteenth floor.

A slim, pale young man wearing a gray gabardine suit let them in. His name was Hopkins, and when Hirschorn introduced Boyle, he shook hands with mechanical vigor. "I've heard a lot about you," he said, his quick eyes appraising Boyle. Boyle knew the type: coolly efficient, impatient of older men, disgruntled at having to work with Q agents.

As they sat down in the room, Hirschorn suggested a drink and a sandwich, which Hopkins refused with a judgmental frown and in obvious petulance shuffled papers in his briefcase when Hirschorn picked up the phone.

"I'm having beer and ham-and-cheese. What about you, Alex?"

"Coffee."

"That all?"

"I'm on a diet. High cholesterol."

"No kidding. Sorry to hear it, Alex. I know how you love a good meal."

"Look," said Hopkins. "We better get started." He waited grimly until Hirschorn had placed the order with room service, then declared, "It's this way," and waited again until both men were looking at him attentively. Then he explained.

It was an explanation that in broad terms Boyle had already anticipated. It was, after all, an old story, compounded of the human errors that he had guessed at in the elevator. The situation had been shaped by arrogance and envy, urged on by the misalliance of men whose training, principles, and goals have little in common. For more than a year an experiment in bacteriological warfare, cosponsored by the Defense and Agriculture Departments, had been conducted on a site chosen for its inaccessibility, on a federal farm in Nevada. Initially, the program had gone well, vindicating their cooperation, and in fact the visiting

131

scientists had achieved a major breakthrough in developing a certain type of weaponry.

Hopkins paused for emphasis. "Unfortunately, there were a few personnel problems."

Imagining only one scene was sufficient for Boyle to translate "personnel problems" into human terms: the cafeteria at noon. Veterinarians seated at their tables, virologists at theirs—fodder discussed on one side of the room, biomathematics on the other, while the ceaseless Nevada wind pushed both groups closer into unacknowledged confrontation. The hatreds breeding and thriving in such an atmosphere were immemorial. Locked together in that desert was the antipathy of country for city, of doer for thinker, of practical engineer for abstract scientist, and the corresponding disdain felt by urbanite intellectuals for men who spend their lives among chickens and sheep.

"All kinds of things went wrong," Hopkins disclosed gloomily, as if the dynamics of such a situation were inexplicable to him, "but only this concerns us: Agriculture refused to have security men on the station, and although the Department compromised by making the station off limits to the general public, the people in charge there turned their heads when the custodians let tour groups stop on Sundays. From what I understand, it was a long-standing practice. Buses stopped and the custodians made some extra money by supplying snacks in the cafeteria."

Hirschorn guffawed, but Hopkins shook his head in disgust.

"I can see those vets laughing," said Boyle, "at the idea of a few old men putting one over on a bunch of elite scientists from Washington."

"Maybe so," Hopkins declared, "but this last Sunday the custodian prepared tea and coffee from poisoned water, and there are a number of water coolers on the station and it was damn hot, which is why the bus stopped in the first place, and those tourists rushed in and in a very real sense drank themselves to death."

"Are you sure they all drank something?" Hirschorn asked.

Hopkins shrugged. "We assume so. We can't waste time finding out if one or two are safe."

Hirschorn turned to Boyle. "You see, Alex, they're still on the bus, happy as clams. At this very moment, according to the schedule, they should be entering Timpie, Utah."

"How was the—" Boyle paused and rather savored the word, "—mistake discovered?"

Hopkins explained that a virologist coming to work this morning had found one of the cages unfastened. Hopkins grimaced. "Initially Defense had separate labs, but Agriculture protested on the grounds that the project called for shared facilities and since the Defense people needed less space than the vets, the labs had to be available to both teams. So now the virologist claims that the vet who shared his lab had tampered with the cages, and the vet swears he hadn't."

"What about the missing mouse?" Boyle asked, unable in spite of the seriousness of the case to stifle a grunt of amusement.

"Took an hour to find it. It was floating outside in the water tank that supplies the whole station. Not only that, but a chlorination check indicated a content slightly too low to kill the microorganisms carried by the mouse." Hopkins lifted his hands in dismay. "Agriculture blames Defense for this, because the potential danger of the experiments made the BW group responsible for safety measures."

"But I suppose Defense claims that Agriculture is responsible because it's their facility."

Hopkins nodded glumly.

"Did employees drink the water, too?" asked Boyle.

"About ten did before the problem was discovered. That

includes the custodian. They've been segregated off the station until we know what to do with them."

"Who's handling the investigation?"

"The local FBI. But they're taking it slow and easy, because both Agriculture and Defense agree it would be a mistake to stir up too much interest, say, in Baker and Ely. Nobody wants a full-scale investigation, certainly not until we deal with the tourists."

"But don't the employees know what happened?"

"Not exactly. They know something went wrong, they definitely know about the mouse, but the vets at least wouldn't understand the ramifications of what happened. They've been briefed, of course, to say nothing."

"*Strongly* briefed?"

"That's my understanding."

"I ask because obviously this station is run like a circus."

"At least the vets don't know how really serious this is. Only the BW people know that and they won't talk."

"How can it be more serious than it already is, with a busload of people dying?"

Hopkins got up. "I think," he said, "you better ask Spitz that." He walked over to a door of the suite and knocked.

A skinny man who seemed to be suffering from extreme fatigue shuffled into the room, rubbing his eyes and yawning. He carried himself gingerly, as if fearful of something breaking, and his singular pallor suggested a grave illness. "Sorry," he mumbled. "The trip from Washington tired me out. Hello, Hirschorn," he said with a wan smile and shook the realtor's hand.

Hirschorn introduced Boyle. "Spitz and I," he told Boyle, "worked together once at Fort Detrick."

"That was an outbreak of Chikungunya Fever, wasn't it?" the pale man said. "We thought it was sabotage, but it was an accident? That's it. Ampules of contaminated yolk sacs were leaking." He lowered himself down on the bed and stretched out with a sigh.

134

"I think we better start," said Hopkins.

"Then start," said Spitz wearily.

"What we've got here," Hopkins began in the measured voice of a lecturer, "is a three-fold problem. First, what do we do about all those tourists? Second, how do we maintain governmental integrity. Third, how do we prevent a national security disclosure of international significance."

"Are you ready for me?" Spitz asked impatiently.

At that moment there was a knock on the door and Hirschorn sprang up. He took a tray from a bellboy and brought it into the room, smiling. "Want anything?" he asked Spitz. "A glass of milk?" Spitz nodded and Hirschorn told the bellboy to bring milk. "And a bourbon for me," he added.

Hopkins glared at the realtor, waited like a schoolteacher until the room was quiet. "I want Spitz to fill you two in, so you fully understand the situation before we make decisions. Go on, Spitz."

Spitz put his hands behind his neck, crossed his feet, and stared up at the ceiling. In a low, shaky voice he described the development of a new bacteriological weapon called Parrot and Pig. It was a mixed agent producing a double disease pattern, its special character being that one mild disease masks the virulence of another. Component One was a virus which produces parrot fever. Its symptoms were pneumonic, but unlike most virus-caused fevers, it responded well to chemotherapy, especially tetracycline. Component Two, called the Pig, came from a spectra of *Brucella* bacteria which normally attack farm animals but which under certain conditions can infect man and produce undulant fever. Undulant fever or brucellosis was merely a debilitating disease, although without proper treatment, it tended to persist for a long time. Recently on the ag station a virologist developed a new strain of *Brucella suis* whose natural host is the common pig. The virologist's mutant was, to put it mildly, a spectacular example of evolution in micro-

135

organisms. It reacted chemically like *Brucella suis*, but established a completely new disease pattern. Instead of producing the general weakness of undulant fever, this mutant strain slowly but surely invaded the lungs of experimental animals much like parrot fever, only with far greater effect. Tetracycline had absolutely no effect on *Brucella suis B*, nor did any other antibiotic. At the present stage of research no antiserum was indicated, and the Pig component proved nearly one hundred percent lethal.

"That's with animals," put in Boyle. "What about with people?"

"Every virologist," said Spitz, "who's looked at the evidence has been convinced that the lethality would be similar." He added with a dry laugh, "This is *one mean pig.*"

"Mean enough to kill off a nation," Boyle observed sourly.

"But not fast enough," Spitz corrected. He explained that unlike plague, which was carried by mobile rats and fleas, P and P was transferred by farm animals. This was the result of life style, almost impossible to change in microorganisms. Any epidemic caused by it would move slowly and modern quarantine methods would quickly halt it.

"We've got much better agents for a full-scale epidemic," Spitz said.

"Well then?"

"Parrot and Pig can be used selectively. Let me explain by posing a hypothetical case." Spitz patted the pillows into shape behind his head and began talking in the thin, hesitant voice of a sick man. He postulated a clinical situation in which a doctor has a patient with pneumonic symptoms that persist, but without severity. Tests indicate parrot fever, so the doctor puts the patient on tetracycline with every expectation of rapid recovery, and indeed, he responds almost immediately. If he has been hospitalized, he might be sent home during this recovery phase. Then the symptoms flare up again, not dangerously so, but they do return, and this recurrence puzzles the doctor because the virus should be under control. On the other hand, the doctor is not going to panic. After all, some strains of an organism are more resistant than others, much like some members of the human race are more resistant to infection than others. He will probably view the return of symptoms as no more than a complication, requiring a little extra work. So the doctor experiments with dosages and supportive combinations of antibiotics, until his lack of success forces him to take additional tests, which reveal the presence of undulant fever. This of course confuses the clinical picture, because now the patient has an illness of both viral and bacterial components. "That," said Spitz, "is the beauty of a mixed agent —it's confusing."

"What you're saying," interjected Boyle, "is that the second bout of the Parrot is really the Pig."

"Exactly. The tetracycline had dealt with the Parrot; the Pig was asserting itself when the symptoms flared up a second time."

"But why hadn't the Pig appeared earlier?"

Spitz lifted his head slightly to have a look at Boyle. "Good question. Because it incubates later than the Parrot. The pre-infectivity period for the Parrot is four to five days, but for the Pig it's about ten."

There was another knock at the door. Hopkins frowned, while Hirschorn took the glass of milk and the bourbon from the bellboy. "Who's got some change?" Hopkins got up quickly and handed the bellboy a dollar.

"Let's continue now," Hopkins fretted.

Spitz explained that even with the complication of undulant fever there is still no cause for alarm, because the disease is typically less serious than parrot fever. But then to the doctor's bewilderment the patient's condition worsens, nothing halts the progress of his deterioration, and within a month he's dead. From lab experiments the end is predictable: a fulminating climax, development of lobular pneumonia marked by rapid breathing of over sixty respira-

137

tions a minute, high temperature, bloody expectoration, edema of the lungs, and convulsions. By then, of course, the hospital has slapped on strict quarantine, because new infections have cropped up among the staff and visitors. For nearly a month, however, the dual nature of Parrot and Pig and the attendant confusion has allowed the slow-moving Pig sufficient time to get a firm grip on a number of victims.

"Let me say something," put in Hopkins. "The point is, this hypothetical patient has been seeing visitors, because, until the last, his condition hasn't warranted quarantine."

"Yes, I see that," said Boyle.

"So Parrot and Pig can be used as a highly selective espionage agent." Hopkins went on with another hypothetical situation. "Through a dairy product you infect an important official of a government and from his hospital room he infects his colleagues who come to pay their respects. Perhaps a few thousand deaths ensue before quarantine procedures halt this sluggish epidemic. But significantly many of the victims have been ruling the nation, and so without decimating the general population an entire government has been crippled by rendering it helpless in the highest echelons.

"Now I see what you mean by a problem of national security," said Boyle. "It would be rather embarrassing for us if this project got into the news."

"Rather," said Hirschorn with a short laugh.

"Other governments know we're attempting something like this, because they are, too," explained Hopkins. "Sooner or later their agents'll find out we have it, but we don't want them to find out through a scandal."

"So our job's to squelch it," Boyle said. "Where do we start?"

The four men stared at each other.

Finally Spitz said, "Let's start with the tourists. By the time their bus returns to San Diego, they'll be hot."

"Tell me this," Boyle said. "When someone dies from this disease, does the Pig die too?"

"No, it's anaerobic, meaning it can live in dead tissue."

"Then how do you kill the Pig?"

"Any number of chemical toxicants will do it. Rubbing alcohol can do the job. You simply break down the hydrogen bonds in the bacterial cell."

"Then can't we kill the Pig without killing the people, too?"

"I'm talking about the kind of chemicals that do *complete* structural damage. When you kill the bacteria in this manner, you get an adverse reaction in the host."

"Meaning?"

"Respiratory arrest and death. *And* a very disagreeable death."

"Since these people are going to die anyway," Boyle said thoughtfully, "couldn't we arrange something painless for them, and after they're dead, take care of the Pig with one of these chemical toxicants?"

"No," Spitz replied firmly. "Once those people are dead, you can't use a toxicant on the Pig. See, at death the blood stagnates. It wouldn't be able to carry the toxicant to the cells."

"I'm ordering another bourbon," Hirschorn announced and went to the phone.

"I'll have a beer now," said Boyle.

"Nothing for me," Hopkins declared primly.

"You can't inject the toxicant *after* they're dead, because it wouldn't kill the Pig. Nothing for me either," said Spitz.

"If we destroyed the bodies, would that kill the Pig?" Boyle asked.

"If you completely destroyed them, yes."

"We could burn them," suggested Hirschorn with his hand clapped over the phone.

"Anything less than complete incineration would be worthless," Spitz warned.

139

"We could put them in a plane with a cargo of inflammables—"

"The whole busload?"

"We could handle the station employees that way."

"I think Hirschorn's got a point there," said Boyle.

"Okay," Spitz said. "But what about the tourists? Incinerating a bus is less sure than a plane. If it didn't burn completely, we'd be back where we started—with enough *Brucella* to contaminate every funeral parlor in San Diego. I think with the tourists the best bet *is* a chemical toxicant."

"Giving it to them while they're still alive?" asked Boyle.

"That's what I mean."

Boyle shook his head. "I don't like it. From what you say, it's one hell of a way to go."

"Do we have a choice?"

"Well, couldn't we put them to sleep first and then give them the toxicant?"

"That's a complication, Alex," Hirschorn said. "We better keep it simple."

"I'm with Boyle," said Spitz. "We could put them to sleep first."

"Wait a minute," Hopkins held up his hand. "Hirschorn is right about simplicity. You know as well as I do that every extra operation increases the margin for error."

"We could plow a gasoline truck into the bus," said Hirschorn.

"But Spitz said if the bodies aren't totally burned, the bacteria are still alive," Boyle argued. "Tour buses are pretty well constructed. What if anyone was thrown clear? And then you've got to get your driver out of the gasoline truck in time. I think it would be a hard thing to stage."

Hopkins nodded.

"Look," said Spitz, "we can anesthetize them and then inject the toxicant. We can use a muscle paralyzant. Let me think." He lay back on the bed, his pale features pinched in concentration. The ice tinkled in Hirschorn's glass. Boyle opened his tobacco pouch and took out a few toasted soybeans.

"What are those?" Hirschorn asked.

"They're my prescribed snack."

"Alex, you're getting old."

"Tricholorethylene," Spitz declared suddenly and rose on his elbows. Then slowly he eased down on the bed again. "No, it wouldn't work. The bus is a closed system."

"I don't get you," said Boyle.

"In a closed system tricholorethylene reacts with oxygen to form a poisonous by-product. That would kill them before you injected the toxicant."

"I'm for the gasoline truck," said Hirschorn.

"That's two of us," said Hopkins.

Another knock at the door had Hirschorn on his feet. Boyle handed him fifty cents as he passed by. He took the tray from the bellboy and returned smiling.

"Here," he said to Boyle, who took the bottle of beer and a glass.

"Fluothane," exclaimed Spitz, raising himself up on his elbows again. "It's a gas with a quick induction phase. You'd knock them out fast. One thing though—the volatility depends on how long it takes the gas to travel through the bus. We better calculate the square feet."

Hopkins wrote this down on a note pad. "I'll see to it."

"We have to deliver the gas quickly or those people might panic," said Boyle. The others nodded. "What about delivery through the air conditioning system?"

"What do you think?" Hopkins asked Spitz.

"I'm no engineer, but I don't think that would be a difficult problem. All you'd need is a timing mechanism and a small charge to trigger it, attached to an aerosol bomb in the A/C unit. You could set it off to the second."

"But when could it be rigged?" asked Boyle.

"I have the bus schedule," said Hopkins, explaining then

141

that the bus would be in Elko tomorrow and in Reno the following day.

"That would be the earliest we could get the thing together," claimed Boyle. "Would the tourists be hot by then?"

"Oh, no," said Spitz. "They wouldn't even be showing symptoms of the Parrot. What's the schedule after Reno?" he asked Hopkins, who explained that after Reno the bus would tour around Lake Tahoe and the Oroville recreation area before arriving in San Francisco that evening.

"By then a few of them would be feeling the Parrot," said Spitz.

"One day in Frisco, then another day's trip to San Diego," Hopkins said.

"At which time they'd all be feeling the Parrot. They'd go home sick to their families. A lot of them would start seeing their doctors. First diagnosis—mild pneumonia. Later—Parrot Fever. And then the Pig hits them and when they begin dying, someone is going to connect their deaths to a certain bus trip."

"But that isn't going to happen, Spitz," said Boyle. "Let's get back to Reno."

The plan soon took shape with the aid of a map that a bellboy got for them in the hotel bookstore. Approximately fifty hours after this meeting, in a Reno garage long after the tourists were asleep, a team of engineers would install a fluothane bomb in the A/C system of the bus and wire the circuit in such a way that the timing device would be activated when the A/C switch was turned on at the dashboard. While the bus was being rigged, the tour driver would be removed from his hotel room. The next morning a substitute would appear and notify the passengers that since the regular driver had suddenly taken ill during the night and was now at the hospital, the tour company had arranged with an affiliate for a replacement. The most complicated phase of the operation would begin after the bus left Reno. After touring around Lake Tahoe and stopping for recreation at Feather Falls, the bus would proceed via Marysville to San Francisco.

Studying the map, Boyle suggested that the gas be activated after the bus left Marysville. "What's that country like, anyway?"

"I know the area," said Hirschorn. "Once I helped a man sell some property around there. It's pretty wild, full of lakes and woods."

"Perfect. We should be able to find a rendezvous spot on the road south of Marysville." Boyle turned to Hopkins. "Can we get a location from the Reno bureau?"

Hopkins nodded and immediately put in a long-distance call.

Boyle munched on some soybeans. "Okay," he mused. "Bus on the road south of Marysville. Our driver turns on the air conditioner. In one minute the gas blows in, and Spitz says we can expect all of them to be asleep in the next."

"Wait," said Hirschorn. "Won't that include our driver?"

"Give him a gas mask," said Spitz. "I can requisition an Olympia. It fits just over the mouth and nose, and you can hold it with one hand. It'll be dark then; none of the passengers will notice."

"Then," said Boyle, "he drives the bus to a rendezvous with the inoculation team. Can you get the people, Spitz?"

Spitz snapped his fingers.

"Their first job is to pump the gas out of the bus, right?"

"They can do it with a rotary pump," Spitz explained. "It carries easily in a pickup truck."

"How long will it take to clear the gas?"

"No more than an hour."

"All right. Next they give the injections."

"I've got him," Hopkins said from the phone. "Colbert? This is Jack Hopkins from Washington. We need a secluded place south of Marysville for a rendezvous. What do you suggest? For a bus and truck. No onlookers. Okay, I'll hold on."

"I've been thinking," Boyle said to Spitz, who was sitting on the bed, looking half asleep. "Can you regulate the time it takes those people to die?"

"We can make it as long or short a time as you want, depending of course to some extent on the constitutional differences of the passengers—age, health, and so on."

"Good," Hopkins said into the phone. "I want to write this down."

"They ought to be dead by the time they reach Frisco," Boyle told Spitz.

"No problem."

"If they die fast, will there be convulsions?"

"Probably. The general rule is, the more powerful the toxicant the more severe the physiological reactions."

"Could you keep them to a minimum?"

Hopkins put the phone down. "We have a rendezvous site," he said. "Colbert swears we won't have any interruptions there."

"Good," Boyle said and turned again to Spitz. "If the convulsions are violent, those people'll be jerking all over the bus and they've got to be driven through Frisco. We want them to look asleep."

"I understand," said Spitz. "I think we can manage to keep convulsions to a minimum."

"Then we're pretty well set. When our driver gets to the second rendezvous on the Coast Road, we put their driver back behind the wheel, and push the bus over the cliff."

"Yes, that's it," Hirschorn agreed and the four men fell silent.

"You're sure this is better than the gasoline truck?" Hopkins said after a while.

"I am," said Boyle.

"I am," said Spitz.

"It's damn complicated," Hirschorn said, "but I'll go along with them."

"Then it's settled," Hopkins declared. "Spitz, you'll take care of the gas and toxicant?"

"Sure, and I'll get the engineers to rig the A/C bomb."

Hopkins turned to Boyle, tapping his pencil on the note pad, like a teacher preparing to admonish a wayward student. "Can you get a driver?"

"Yes, I can."

"One of your *boys?*" Hopkins drawled. "You see, I've heard of them."

"Have you?" said Boyle.

"He's had plenty of success with them," put in Hirschorn in the soothing tone of a man accustomed to arranging compromises.

"It's my personal opinion," said Hopkins loftily, "using criminals is a dangerous procedure."

"Some of the best people I ever worked with have been criminals," Boyle said.

"Oh, I understand how you Q agents think."

"If we didn't think the way we do," countered Boyle, "there wouldn't be any need for us."

"All right, get your driver. Keep yourself available in Frisco if anything goes wrong."

"Of course."

"Hirschorn, will you handle the Coast Road phase?"

"No problem. I know three Q agents who'll do the job just fine."

"Q agents?" Hopkins smiled sourly. "Don't you employ hoods like Boyle here?"

Hirschorn repeated his words in a measured tone of repressed annoyance. "I know three Q agents who'll do the job just fine."

"I'm sure they will," said Hopkins. "They get *paid* enough. All you Q agents and Boyle's criminals are going to break the bank yet." With a triumphant smile he looked

145

down at his note pad, while Boyle and Hirschorn exchanged knowing glances. Funding for Q operations and indeed the very concept of such operations had prompted many regulars in the field to complain bitterly about such agents. If malcontents like Hopkins had their way, reasoned Boyle as he watched the young man writing on the pad in a precise hand, what had happened on the Nevada hog farm would occur with equally disastrous results within the nation's intelligence system.

"I'll coordinate from Washington," Hopkins said, looking up finally. "Boyle, if you need to contact me, do it through Hirschorn. Spitz, we better get the next plane back."

The pallid man nodded wearily, then his eyes, brilliant from the look of fever, turned toward Boyle. "There's one more problem," he said breathing in short, panting gusts. "What are you going to do about your driver?" In answer to Boyle's quizzical expression, Spitz explained that even though the Pig's incubation phase would not be completed at the time of the tourists' deaths, conceivably the driver could still pick up the infection because of long exposure to it inside the bus. This was especially true because the bus was a closed system in which he would be breathing for many hours.

"I'm not saying it's probable, but it sure is possible," Spitz concluded. "Your driver could catch the Pig."

After a long silence, Boyle said, "What you imply is, he'll have to be eliminated after the job."

"At last I can see the function of your boys," Hopkins acknowledged sarcastically. "If someone's expendable, it might as well be a cheap hood."

Boyle glared at him. "Or Q agents, right, Hopkins?" He turned to Spitz before the young man could reply. "Should it be done?"

Spitz shrugged. "Like I say, it's possible but not probable he'll get the Pig. The odds? Who knows. Maybe one in ten, maybe more."

"But the fact is, it would be good insurance," Boyle speculated.

"It would, Alex," Hirschorn agreed. "Otherwise, it's a loose end."

"How should it be done?" Boyle asked Spitz.

"Well," the sick man pursed his lips, "that's up to you. Only however you do it, make sure to burn the body. If you don't, we're back where we started. The coroner, attendants in the morgue—they'd all be probables."

"Any special method of incineration?"

"Any will do. Kerosene, for example. Just so the tissues are destroyed."

Hopkins closed his note pad with a smack of finality. "Then that's it." He got to his feet. "We better get going. That bus is carrying the worst load of publicity this country has faced in a long time."

Hands were shaken all around, and Boyle left the suite in Hirschorn's company. They were silent on the elevator, as a smartly dressed woman eyed Boyle with mild appreciation. In the lobby Boyle said, "That Hopkins is a sonofabitch."

"Yes," Hirschorn admitted with a chuckle, "but he gets the job done. He's one of the rising lights. He sure doesn't care much for us old-timers, does he? Did you see his face when you told him Q agents were expendable? He was really pissed off."

"But it's the truth."

"Of course. I just don't think he liked the idea of us being so *glamorous* at our age."

They shook hands, and as they parted, Hirschorn turned to say, "What did you think of Spitz?"

"I liked him."

"Yeah, but he sure is sick. How in hell does he keep going? I can remember him a few years ago, vigorous as they come."

"We're all getting old," Boyle said.

147

"Maybe so, but we're still more creative than a lot of these new people like Hopkins."

"That's age talking."

They both grinned and walked off, taking separate ways out of the Saint Francis.

8

Drowsy a few thousand feet above California, bound for San Francisco and a final confrontation with Victoria Welch, he recalled that meeting in the Saint Francis Hotel. In a hypnagogic state between waking and sleeping, Boyle reassembled the operation into a mosaic of clearer meaning. It would have been successful had *he* not failed. If only he had checked the bus! Now the personal property of forty dead people was missing and in a publicized inquiry, abetted by an energetic press that Watergate had taught to suspect anything, who knows where the public lust for scandal might lead? Boyle could imagine the headlines screaming it: GOVERNMENT PROJECT DOOMS TOURISTS! And from Moscow to Peking, from London to New Delhi, there would be laughter as well as consternation. In Washington the gears of investigation would grind into mesh, and a host of officials would scramble to be first with the embarrassing surmises, the sensational disclosures, the righteous accusations—in fact, everything that he had been dedicated to prevent, ever since becoming a Q agent. For Alexander Boyle and for Q agents like him, there were two kinds of people in the world: Those who made a mess and those who

149

cleaned it up. In government there were plenty of mess makers who imperiled the public health, so it was the special task of a dedicated few to keep the nation from stinking. That's how Boyle saw himself—as a sanitation engineer. He never carried a broom or a bucket of disinfectant, he never wore a uniform or a billed cap, he never emptied trash baskets or unclogged drains, but his job was sanitation just the same. Even before joining the Q force ten years ago, when he had still been an agent of the FBI, he had proudly thought of himself as a sanitation man. When at his wife's insistence he had quit the bureau, Boyle had been easily persuaded to keep his commitment alive by working with the Q force. So in giving up the FBI to pursue the peaceful life his Cora had always wanted for him, he had joined a unit whose work was far more dangerous. Cora would not have enjoyed the grim irony of it. For Boyle, on the other hand, it was the ultimate commitment, because the Q force was a profound experiment in national security. The concept had developed quite logically from the CIA practice of installing its overseas agents in business organizations, in embassies, and even in the armed forces. Why not use a similar method at home? Why not enlist former military people and other ex-government employees and in some instances patriotic men from the business and scientific communities to protect the national image from within? The very arguments against such a plan—it was illegal, lawless, unaccountable to the public—were precisely its strengths. In exceptionally sensitive situations it was obviously profitable to employ operatives who would not trace back to official command; what they did, they did as private citizens, with no visible connection to the government their actions might embarrass. Funding the program was easily hidden within the jungle of appropriations for intelligence work, and as long as the unswerving loyalty of its agents was assured, the only people who stood to lose were the agents themselves. Perhaps thirty or forty men in the whole nation comprised this tight-knit unit. Pride in their work and faith in its importance had been their compensation, and thus far, in the dozen years of the Q force's existence, not a single agent had divulged, either consciously or accidentally, his role in the nation's intelligence system. For some, of course, the compensation was as much monetary as emotional—funds paid for a job had kept more than one of them afloat in his business career—but for Boyle and others like him it was enough that the nation's reputation sometimes depended upon their skill to protect it.

And now he had jeopardized that reputation by making a mistake worthy of an amateur.

He sat up with a sudden jerking motion and waved to the stewardess. "Double whiskey," he said and watched her trim figure retreating, his mind filled for a moment with the image of Julie Saunders. He basked in a daydream: They were on this plane together, only it was not bound for San Francisco but for Hong Kong and sunsets on the terrace of the Repulse Bay Hotel from which vantage point they could watch the Chinese junks heading for the bay and touch the rims of their Pimms Cups in a romantic toast. The whiskey came and he bolted it, feeling lousier than ever. Since leaving Salt Lake City a strange fatigue, a powerful lethargy had settled over him. Perhaps his incredible mistake accounted for this feeling. Why, why, why had he sat all snug in his car for a full ten minutes only twenty feet away from his duty, where Tony Aiello fixed the engine, and the dead passengers sat upright in attitudes of drowsiness against the windows? What had been in his mind during those fateful ten minutes? Had he been tired? Chilled by the morning air? He couldn't remember being distracted by anything, except those faces inside the bus, those ghostly faces swimming up from the depths of night. It occurred to him now that in a strange way they had surfaced from the past, from the Iowa of his childhood. He had seen people just like them in buses back in Iowa: shopkeeper and grandmother, student and farmer, mechanic and bride, traveling from one small community to another, drawn by decent business or family need across the rolling plains of the Midwest. In a withering moment of awareness Alexander Boyle understood how he had confused a memory and the present. No wonder he hadn't crossed the street to view his handiwork, no wonder he'd avoided walking up that aisle. He had been *spooked*.

Such things happened to the best of professionals; men noted for solid performance suddenly made inexplicable errors and, when called to account, merely shook their heads in bewilderment. Not stupidity but genuine lapses in concentration had caused the mistakes—the phenomenon was recognized by anyone who lived dangerously. Often such inattentiveness came from a momentary surrender to wayward memory, to something inconsequential, to something forgotten for years, to a face, an object, a sensation. Boyle had heard men talk of being spooked in this fashion, and in their recital they had always seemed mystified, even humbled, as if the paralyzing power of such an event defied analysis. In his own career, Alexander Boyle had never been spooked, but now he must face the dismaying probability that finally it had happened to him, too.

There was a pressure on his arm and he looked up to focus on the pretty face of a stewardess, who told him again to fasten his seat belt. "We're coming into San Francisco."

Opening the window curtain, Boyle squinted down at the glittering blue bay and the white buildings. Minutes later he was filing along with other passengers down the ramp.

A stewardess cast an admiring glance at the tall man descending. He looked like someone who caused things to happen, on whose judgment people depended. Too bad he had dozed most of the flight. Too bad she hadn't met him.

In an airport phone booth he called Hirschorn.

"They're damned upset in Washington," Hirschorn exclaimed immediately.

"Yes, well, I'm on my way now."

"Keep us informed, Alex."

"Us?"

"Hopkins is giving me hell. He wants to know exactly what you're doing."

"You tell Hopkins I know what I'm doing. Twenty-five years I've known what I'm doing." Boyle didn't wait for Hirschorn's attempt at conciliation, but hung up and then called the gallery.

It was strange, but even now, in the midst of the worst of it, he could think of his other profession.

The line was busy. Young Vertrees was probably sitting with his feet propped up on the desk, conducting a love affair. Boyle went into the men's room and rented a dressing stall. He took the Webley & Scott from his luggage, checked the mechanism, loaded it, turned its weighty efficient-looking shape in his hand, then shoved it into his belt holster. He glared at the mirror and glaring back at him was the pale haggard face of a stranger who looked haunted, sick, the edge of his eyes pinched in concentration, his mouth open like a tired dog's. Boyle placed widespread hands on his belly and probed gently, like a physician. He had gained weight in the last week—probably more than five pounds, most of it from fatty meat and booze. That's what came of taking on such a job. He stored his suitcase in a locker, then called the gallery again. This time Vertrees answered.

"What's going on?" Boyle asked crisply.

"Well, Mr. Denver called. He wants a Goldstoff oil for the museum show."

"Which one?"

"The big one—'Flight.'"

"Tell him okay. Call right now, because Denver tends to change his mind, and I want Goldstoff represented in that

153

show. 'Flight' is a good choice, too. Have you heard from Kawabata?"

"No. But Di Mattio called and wants to see you."

Boyle warmed to the conversation. He was talking art now. It was as if his mind was a railroad switchyard where a slight shifting of track could send energy instantly in a new direction. His ideas went full steam ahead into his other world. "Di Mattio," he said, "is a pain in the ass. His last show didn't sell because it lacked quality, but he wants to blame everybody but himself. Tell him I'll call when I can. Anything else?"

"I sold two Oppenheim serigraphs."

"Good. That'll encourage him. Who bought them?"

"Let me see—a Mrs. Kogut."

"Don't know her. Anything else?"

There was a pause. "Miss Saunders called again."

"Anything else?" Boyle asked gruffly.

"She called three times."

"I want you to contact Kawabata today," Boyle said. "Tell that wife of his if I don't see a new painting by next Monday, I'm canceling his show. Don't let it bother you if she says she doesn't understand. She understands all right."

"Is anything wrong, Mr. Boyle?"

"No. Why?" Boyle demanded sharply. "Why do you ask me that?"

"Well, I don't know. The sound of your voice—"

"The sound of my voice?"

"It just sounds different."

"I am *tired*, Vertrees. Is *that* sufficient explanation?" He added quickly, "I may not be in tomorrow. Can you handle it?"

"I can," the young man said.

Boyle said good-bye and hung up, furious at himself for losing his temper. And yet it was unlike Vertrees to ask a personal question. Tone of voice was hardly the sort of thing to which that young man would respond—unless it

154

was the voice of romance. Vertrees was efficient, but hardly sensitive to the emotions of people not involved in his own intrigues. Still, Boyle shouldn't have lost control. Cora would have blamed his outburst on the present job. He could imagine her saying querulously but in the resigned tone of a long-suffering wife, "You can't be an art dealer and a government agent both. It will make you bitter." As usual she would be on target, and yet he suspected that his flare-up was more complicated than mere petulance.

He left the airport, carrying with him the deliciously painful knowledge that Julie Saunders was still calling. When this was all over—he began to lapse into a daydream of them together, as he stood at the curb waiting for a taxi. He shot his gaze upward at the brilliant sky to break his concentration on her. He mustn't act like a love-struck adolescent, certainly not now, when the entire case was rushing toward a climax. A taxi came and Boyle gave the driver Victoria Welch's address, then sat back and repeated to himself those curious words just uttered by Mr. Vertrees: "Is anything wrong, Mr. Boyle?" It wasn't like Vertrees. What Boyle had especially admired in his assistant was detachment, a commitment to life outside the gallery. But then, what did he really know about the young man, except that he displayed a solid knowledge of art, dealt well with clients, and furtively made phone calls? Boyle had hired him more than a year ago on Hirschorn's recommendation. Boyle's last assistant had left to get married, and on their last case together, involving the elimination of a Q agent, he had told Hirschorn of his need for a replacement at the gallery. Hirschorn had recommended Vertrees, a former college friend of his son's. Hirschorn had recommended him, which in retrospect was quite a coincidence. Quite a coincidence.

While the taxi sped into the city, Boyle let himself go and allowed his mind the freedom to construct a fantastic theory. Hirschorn had recommended Vertrees in order to place someone in the gallery who might prove valuable, who if the need arose could do the work of a spy. It was not impossible, certainly, and in view of Pentagon touchiness about Q agents anyway, it was probable that at one time or another all of them were checked for competence, for trustworthiness. Had Hopkins, for example, ordered *him* to place someone in Hirschorn's real estate company, Boyle would have obeyed the young sonofabitch without hesitation. After all, both he and Hirschorn were Q agents and that made them totally vulnerable. Q agents. No doubt some little man buried deep within the Pentagon, paid to think up code names the way failed poets were paid to think up Burma Shave jingles in another age, had thought of the label Q—Q for quasi, defined as "resembling but not being the thing in question." And it was an appropriate label, because people like himself and Hirschorn were not agents, officially, but resembled agents only in taking dangerous assignments. Ultimately they were expendable, just as he had reminded Hopkins. It was altogether possible, and on second thought even probable, that Hirschorn had planted young Vertrees on either explicit or implicit order from one of those faceless, nameless operators who manipulated the Q force agents, like puppets on a string, from an innocuous little office in the Pentagon.

Viewed in this light the languishing air of Mr. Vertrees was not that of a problem-beset young lover but of a rather awkward amateur spy.

Ahead, through the taxi window, Boyle saw Victoria Welch's apartment house, ragged clapboard, stained with gull droppings, and once again he felt that everything about the woman was incongruous. Who would expect a proper librarian to live in such a hovel down by the waterfront, among stevedores and drifters? In her red pillbox hat and thick glasses, her figure stereotypically dumpy, she looked the part of someone who lived with books and believed in astrology, and at the same time she had the sharp eyes of

156

a trained investigator, the resoluteness of a marine. Her apartment possessed none of the mementos of a lonely aging woman, except one—a photo album revealing intense involvement in family life. Her conversation was pleasantly commonplace, yet she had within herself the passionate vision of a zealot, who in a moment's resolve was capable of setting out on impossible missions. What would he do with such a woman? Persuade or threaten her? And with what? To offer her money for the goods would only disgust her and stiffen her resolve. To threaten her even with death would merely have the same effect. He must persuade her by appealing to her own idealistic temperament.

Boyle paid the driver and mounted the stairs, his nostrils filling with the pungent odor of fish. For a moment he stopped and held on to the banister—what if she didn't have the property or even know where it was? That was still possible. He was certain of only one thing: Victoria Welch had returned to protect the stolen property. What he must learn was the extent to which she understood its significance and her plans for its disposal. Whether she lived or died within the hour would depend on those answers.

Walking up to her door, he took a deep breath and knocked briskly.

A muffled sound came from within, then the door opened, and Victoria Welch stood there in a faded housecoat, her small blue eyes enlarged behind glasses, a thick book in her pudgy hand.

"Come in," she said in the flat tone of someone opening the door for a grocery boy. "I thought it might be you."

She had been waiting for an hour with *Crime and Punishment* in her lap and a brisk black tea called Iron Goddess of Mercy on the table next to her chair. She had expected Mr. Boyle or someone like him to come. She was ready, and as she ushered him into the room, she hoped that her demeanor showed it.

157

"Would you like a cup of tea?" she asked coolly. "If you'd like something stronger, I keep Scotch for visitors."

"Scotch, please."

She was astonished by the man's appearance. He seemed to have aged perceptibly in the last day. Seated in the leather chair that Henry had loved so much, Mr. Boyle looked alarmingly like her own grandfather, who had been an army colonel. There was a likeness in the way Mr. Boyle sat with both feet planted as if taking root, hands flat on his knees, his lips tight and inscrutable. For a moment the similarity between this man and her grandfather awed, even frightened her, but then shrugging off the spell of remembered authority she went into the kitchen for the whiskey. She found the bottle behind some spices and poured an inch of the Scotch into a thick glass (superb crystal, the lone survivor of a wedding set) and took it to him.

She noticed his hand tremble slightly when he reached for the glass, and this pleased her. She wanted him to squirm, and in daydreams during her flight back to San Francisco, she had relished the idea of him coming to her apartment puzzled and desperate. The fear she had felt during her wait for that knock on the door had been nothing compared to her growing sense of triumph. Justice for her nephew, justice for all those other people, too, would begin to take place here in her apartment, among memories of her family. She sat down in the chair opposite Mr. Boyle and watched him raise the glass to his lips. At that moment she said, "It was my boss, old Sackman, who gave you away." She saw with pleasure how his face twisted suddenly in surprise. "Yes, it was Sackman. You compared her to someone who was *also* a nonstop talker. Now I thought that was peculiar, because I hadn't told you *she* was. I realized then you'd met her." She paused, waiting for him to comment, but when he didn't she continued. "So I knew you were on my trail." She was aware from the man's faint smile that he considered her way of expressing herself rather melodramatic, perhaps old-fashioned, but she went on. "It was obvious then that you'd joined the tour because of me."

"You are absolutely right."

She was disappointed by his ready admission, having hoped for a denial that she could counter. It was Taurean of him to be frank. On the other hand, Machiavelli had the same birthdate, and she had no idea of other planetary influences on Mr. Boyle because she hadn't made his chart. She was certain of one thing: His cold eye was Arien, the sign of blood and violence.

"I'm going to be frank with you, too," she said.

"That would be best."

"You joined the tour hoping to learn from me where the property was that my nephew stole."

"I'm still interested in it, Miss Welch."

"Hear me out. One way or another I've come to the conclusion that the so-called bus accident has something to do with the agricultural station we stopped at in Nevada."

"Let's discuss the property."

For a moment she was afraid—this man was a cool customer who might outwit her, although justice was on *her* side. She decided to draw back and let him do the leading for a while. "All right, Mr. Boyle, discuss the property."

"Do you have it?"

"I do." She gripped the arms of the chair and leaned toward him, saying breathlessly, "But you'll never get one watch, one bracelet, one billfold of it from me!"

"Where is it, Miss Welch?"

"In safekeeping."

"I see."

"No, you *don't* see. It's in two safety-deposit boxes and has been ever since Warren was murdered." She rejoiced to see the man frown at this news. "Moreover, today when I returned I mailed the keys in a letter to my lawyer. If anything should happen to me, he has instructions to read that letter and open the safe-deposit boxes."

"Letter?"

"I'm convinced there's enough in it to start an investigation. Mr. Boyle, why are you smiling?"

"Am I? I was thinking of the safety-deposit boxes. Simple but effective."

"I'm an average citizen, Mr. Boyle. All I know about these things is what I read in books and see in movies. But I know one thing, and that's the real value of the stolen property."

"Which is, Miss Welch?"

"Sentiment, Mr. Boyle. The relatives of those poor people will want that property back. That's the way families are, Mr. Boyle. You can't put them off forever and you know it. You couldn't say it was stolen, unless you admitted those passengers had been robbed *after* they were dead but *before* the accident. If you did that, the trail would lead back to Baker, Nevada. Now *I* have the property and I intend to see that such a thing *does* happen. Mr. Boyle!" She leaned forward in alarm. The man's face, ashen as old newsprint, was twitching and his hand shot to his chest. For an instant it was as if her own husband's heart attack were being reenacted before her eyes, and she leaped to her feet. "Mr. Boyle!"

Staring straight ahead, he grimaced, crushing the material of his jacket with both fists.

"Is it your heart?" She hovered over him, seeing in a terrible flashing image her Henry writhing on the floor.

The man's eyes focused on her, for a few more seconds he gasped like a fish thrown up onshore, then slowly his hand relaxed and dropped to his side.

"Is it your *heart*, Mr. Boyle?" She glanced at the phone.

"No," the man said faintly. He took a deep breath and said again, "No."

She stood above him, clasping and unclasping her hands, speaking in a low voice as much for herself as for him. "My

160

husband was just about your age, a Libra with his moon in Taurus. I am *convinced* the Taurean moon was what killed him—he ate too much, he worked too hard. He was a wonderful man who cared for others while neglecting himself, he—" She paused and noticed with astonishment that the man was weakly smiling. Then she understood why. She was speaking to him like a friend. It was supremely incongruous.

"I'm fine now," he said. "Gastritis. Just that. I'm prone to it—" he motioned at the empty glass, "when I drink."

She sat down, shaken by the memory of her husband lying on the floor in the white heat of agony. Softly she said, "Have you ever really loved anyone, Mr. Boyle?"

"I told you once before. Yes." He took a deep breath, ran his fingertips across his sweating brow.

"I believe you. It's typical of your sign. Taureans are under the influence of Venus. Yes, I believe you, but you're terribly hard, too. You're callous, Mr. Boyle. You could kill me right now without a qualm. Maybe I understand that. I loved my nephew, but I haven't shed one tear for him, and I won't until justice's been done. I could see you die with pleasure, Mr. Boyle."

"*Vengeance is mine; I will repay, saith the Lord.*"

"*You* quote that," she scoffed.

"I don't think," he said, "in my entire life I ever did anything in the spirit of revenge." He added with a smile, "Is that Taurean?"

"As a matter of fact, no. And anyway, what I'm seeking is justice, not revenge." She felt the heat rising to her cheeks.

"Are you sure?"

"How can *you*, a cold-blooded murderer—"

"That's a wild assumption, Miss Welch."

"But a reasonable one! A murderer—you or someone like you. I don't know exactly what happened out there in the desert, but I can make an educated guess. Some sort of experiment went wrong and those tourists either found out about it or got hurt by it. That's for someone else to discover. All I know is you and people with you have been trying to cover up some terrible mistake. You've been ready to go to any lengths—" Victoria was breathing heavily, aware she was on the edge of control. The last time she had cried had been after her husband's funeral, in the sanctity of her room. But she was almost crying now, from anger and frustration.

The man leaned slightly forward, his face calmly speculative like an inquiring physician. "Miss Welch," he said, "do you love your country?"

"Love my country? Of course I do."

"Enough to defend it with your own life?"

"I would hope so."

"You're saying, then, a man who loves his country should be willing to protect it."

"And what you're saying is simplistic, Mr. Boyle. Nothing justifies killing innocent people. Nothing. One individual life—"

"I know the argument," he cut in. "But what if soldiers used it in combat?"

"You're not a soldier. I don't know exactly what you are, but you're not a soldier."

"Anyone who defends his country is a soldier. Let's assume I'm doing that now and if I do I'm as much of a soldier as I was on the beaches of Normandy."

Victoria realized that the point of his argument went beyond the philosophical justification of killing. He was trying to tell her that her own deduction, one so terrible that she had thus far refused to deal with it directly, was quite possibly true: Boyle and his confederates were in some despicable way working *to protect the government*. It was incredible, but the facts seemed to support that conclusion. Here and now she couldn't face the ramifications of such a dismaying possibility. She decided to act as if Mr. Boyle's role in this affair, though vital to it, was a vague, ultimately inexplicable one which better minds than hers must examine. She would play the ostrich with its head in the sand. She would debate with him, but only in theory, and swerve clear of what in actuality he implied.

"In the war," she said, "you killed soldiers, not innocent people."

"Civilians die in war. Until Vietnam we all seemed to accept that fact."

"So you condone that, too."

"I'm condoning nothing. Even if the war had been a popular one, more easily justified, those same civilians would have been killed."

Victoria took a deep breath, shaken by the exchange which her daydream of justice had not prepared her for. She wished suddenly that her husband was there, who would have countered with surer logic, but about *one* thing she knew she was right and said so. "There's no justification for killing the innocent. There never is."

"Even if the security of your country is involved?"

"No."

"But soldiers who are drafted and go to war and get killed, aren't they innocent?"

"That's a specious argument."

"Let me pose a hypothetical situation. What if those people on the bus were going to die anyway? Let's say they were doomed to a terrible death and with—some help, they could die without pain."

"That's not your choice to make."

"—with the added advantage of protecting the reputation of the country."

"Reputation!"

"Would you still say there wasn't a gray area of morality involved?"

She hesitated before replying. Like a true Taurean the man was persistent and in a way persuasive. But he was wrong, wrong, wrong, and she heard herself screaming,

"You killed my nephew, you or someone like you killed Warren in cold blood! You murdered him!"

The man was on his feet, his face waxy and pinched, years older than it had been yesterday.

"What are you doing?" she shouted, as he stood there, hands at his side, his eyes dull and lusterless.

"I'm going."

"Then—that's all?"

"We're at an impasse, you and I. What you're contemplating won't bring your nephew back, but it could hurt the country that has clothed and fed you, that you *say* you'd defend with your life. That simple little device of mailing a letter to a lawyer—you've won with it." He turned and started for the door, muttering as he went, "You'll have your revenge."

"Not revenge. Justice!" She was on her feet too. "He was murdered in cold blood. Doesn't that *mean* anything to you? Don't you see?" She watched in dismay as he put his hand on the doorknob. "Don't go!"

He turned and looked at her, his stony face set in the kind of reproach that she could remember from her childhood, when grandfather disapproved.

"We must—" she said faintly, "talk more."

"Now?"

"Tomorrow. Come back tomorrow. I'll convince you that what you've done is wrong. I will. I know it."

"Would my coming tomorrow prevent you from turning the property in?"

"No."

"You see? We're at an impasse."

She watched the door open and then close behind his tall broad-shouldered figure, and in the waning light she sat motionless until the evening moved into the room and left her in darkness. Opposite her was the black bulk of the empty chair. It was certain that the man would not come back tomorrow, although she hoped desperately that he

164

would. She had a vision of them sitting over this problem again. How far should men go to protect their country and at what human cost? But it was an abstract question compared to the deaths of those people. Even if they had been going to die, someone else had decided exactly when and how. That was wrong. And her nephew had not been one of them. Warren had died merely because of what he knew, and that was wrong. The man who had just left her apartment had probably murdered Warren. A stranger had decided that her own flesh and blood must die. That was wrong. It was wrong no matter how many arguments were used to compare foreign and domestic war. Life was one-to-one. She would have *revenge* for *one* death. And yet this revenge suddenly seemed hollow and, perhaps in some inexplicable way, she would pay for it the rest of her life. Tomorrow when she called her lawyer and released the letter, Alexander Boyle and men like him would be exposed to the merciless glare of morality nurtured on comfortable living and blind habit and self-righteousness. Her actions would brand men like Alexander Boyle as monsters, and in a sense they were. They would be humiliated, vilified, and disgraced, and in a sense they should be. They had committed the ultimate public sin by playing God with the welfare of people whose laws they thought they were protecting. Like all fanatics they were pathetic, a menace to society, and yet like all fanatics they were admirable in their resoluteness. The man Boyle had won a kind of victory— he had upset her belief in the clarity of what was right.

Slowly she rose from her chair, turned on the light, and shuffled into the kitchen. She would have the finest of Japanese greens. Drawing cold water from the tap, Victoria put on the kettle and from a row of teas in the cabinet, she selected the pale leaf of Pearl Dew. She needed steadying. The man had called her sense of justice a desire for revenge, and perhaps he was right. Very well, along with the tea she would savor her revenge. By tomorrow evening whole sectors of the government might be implicated in an astonishingly callous plot. Her reasons for bringing this about no longer mattered. Her nephew's death cried out for it and so did the deaths of all those other people. If she knew one thing, she knew that killing innocent people is never justified, that life transcends the logic of morality. And yet she also understood that because of her actions tomorrow, she might very well be deciding the fate of numerous public servants, who were unconvinced of wrongdoing, and by this decision she would become one in spirit with Alexander Boyle, linked to him by the kind of commitment that shakes nations.

9

Outside in a dazzle of sunlight Alexander Boyle paused
and glanced up at the open window of Victoria Welch's
apartment. He felt exhausted, sweat rolled from his face,
and the gastritis still twitched in his chest. The audacity
of the woman, taking on the entire government! Yet he admired her courage, despite his contempt for idealists who
with their fuzzy morality were capable of walking through
fire to prove it didn't exist. How effortlessly such people
could obstruct the processes that protected their right to be
obstructive. Did they think the analysis of conduct was a
simple matter of right and wrong? Long ago he had left the
unraveling of moral knots to those with the leisure for it.

And yet the plump librarian with her tea and astrology
had unnerved him, just as his wife had managed to do, both
of them arguing that the commitment which had given his
life meaning was ultimately criminal. And Victoria Welch
had nearly succeeded in convincing him, whereas Cora had
failed throughout their marriage. Perhaps the librarian's success was a function of his age. But he had better guard
against introspection—the disease of the amateur. What

167

should be uppermost in his mind was the failure of his mission.

He moved slowly down the sunlit street, slogging through the warm air as if his feet were sucking through mud. He was tired and depressed, shot through with a growing sense of failure. And it was success and failure that counted, not theory, not abstract morality, not the sorrowful righteousness of a woman he had loved and not the outrage of a woman he had learned to respect. He called Hirschorn from a booth, described the interview, and acknowledged that he had failed. There was nothing more he could do. Victoria Welch had won.

"I agree," Hirschorn said after a long pause. "I think Hopkins will agree, too. I'll call him and get back to you. Will you be at home?"

"Either there or the gallery."

"Alex, how are you taking it?"

"What do you mean how am I taking it?" Boyle laughed.

"Don't get sore."

"Okay so I'm just taking it. There's nothing else possible."

"That's the spirit. I'll get back to you."

Perhaps Hirschorn would "get back to him" or perhaps send Vertrees, imitating his own practice of using outsiders, like Tony Aiello. Both he and Hirschorn had always known that their work was so delicate, so fraught with consequence, that a significant blunder could make either of them expendable. They had fully accepted the philosophy that a country must, if it could, rid itself of patriots whose errors are embarrassing. From the moment that he had taken on this assignment, voluntarily and in full knowledge of what he was doing, the responsibility for success or failure had been his. It had always been a source of pride for him and for sanitation men like him that they either cleaned up the mess or became part of the mess themselves. Even as he walked down this blustery street among decent citizens bound for home, there were men somewhere in windowless

168

offices who were discussing what to do with him, as if he were a commodity to buy or sell. The assignment which he and Hirschorn had shared before this last one—he recalled it now, its pertinence obvious. A Congressman had been suspected of taking bribes from contractors, not for his own aggrandizement but for philanthropies in a foreign town where his relatives still lived. The idea was to suppress his activities by confronting him (more fool than criminal) with evidence of a misguided generosity. The Q agent sent to find such evidence among papers in the Congressman's home was a former marine and then a gas station owner in Sacramento. He found no evidence, but he spooked, shot the maid who discovered him at his search and he was seen leaving the house by a delivery boy. Not only that, the maid survived to give her own description of him. The enraged Congressman, convinced that the entire nation was in the grip of wholesale violence because a single thief had chosen his home to rob, caused such a stir at the Pentagon that Justice agents were forced to make an intensive investigation. They worked from the two eyewitness accounts, which described the man's approximate size and age and most importantly an unusual disfigurement: a withered left ear. Once it was established that the man had no police record, the FBI would doubtlessly make a computer check of military files, using that withered ear as the focus for data search. Sooner or later the Q agent whose ear had been burned like a dry leaf by a Korean flame thrower, would be hunted down by a division of the security establishment which had hired him to commit the burglary in the first place and which had unofficially licensed him to prevent detection by any means.

So Boyle and Hirschorn had been brought into the situation, their job to lure him to an airport where other people (Boyle had no idea if they were Q agents or CIA or DIA men or operatives from yet another elite group whose existence was perhaps known to less than a dozen top officials) would take care of him. Hirschorn's job was to get him into the parking lot; there Boyle sapped him unconscious, and both of them delivered him to an ambulance waiting in the darkness. Later, from the observation deck of the airport, they stood together for a last view of a man with whom they had worked for the good of the nation: A heavily bandaged patient accompanied by a male nurse was wheeled by stretcher to a plane bound for the Orient. Hirschorn didn't disclose the details of the operation, but Boyle could guess. Listed as an American businessman with a terminal illness returning to his adopted country, the man was going to have a drugged flight across the Pacific and within a few days his corpse, throat slit or bearing burn marks or slashes of torture, would appear in a river or gutter or back alley, bearing in his shoe or coat lining some false documents which would hopefully fall into the right hands and convince either friend or foe that he had been a United States agent, killed in the line of duty, carrying information that would prove anything our intelligence people wanted to have proved. Something like that. His fate would be a variation on that basic theme. He would serve his country one last time with a death fortuitous and useful. Boyle had approved of the procedure then and still approved of it now, even though his own fate was now in the balance. It was, after all, the occupational hazard of a sanitation man. And yet he hated to end his own career like a fine athlete who bumbles into retirement by losing a game in full view of teammates who respect him.

A group of young people swept past laughing, one of them jostling him without knowing it. He glanced over his shoulder at them, envying their closeness. It occurred to him that commitment had walled him off from people. But perhaps any profession was a closed system of ritual and habit, walling its members off from the rest of society. Cora alone had really understood him, but now she was gone, and he felt like an alien in his own country. He halted and looked back again, seeing the young backs tented together, hands clasping hands, young voices rising above the clang of an ascending trolley, and he thought of Julie Saunders, who in the midst of his present anxieties had almost given him the hope of a new future. He stopped in a bar for a quick beer, hunched over it in the dim, cosy glow through which people at leisure were moving with the casual gestures of contentment. He drank the beer, more aware than ever of his isolation. He knew what dedication felt like in the blood. When commitment took hold of you, the result was like electrodes feeding jolts of electricity through your body; you moved to impulses not your own. The work channeled and defined your life until whatever that work was, you were, too, for most of the day. You shared its obsessions, you saw life through it, except that he had been in the heady but confusing position of having two professions, two commitments. He thought of the *other* one and left the bar. Hailing a cab, he drove out to the Kawabata studio. He knocked sharply on the door, and Mrs. Kawabata opened it. Seeing him, she bowed low, but stood in the doorway, so that Boyle had to brush past her. It was too late for the artist to escape behind the screen—he lurched up from the lacquered table and approached unsteadily, his wrinkled face all wreathed in smiles. Turning away from the little man's extended hand, Boyle said to the woman, "Did my assistant call you today?"

"Oh, yes, Mr. Broyle, oh, yes."

Boyle was then pulled into the middle of the studio by the little artist's strong hands.

"See?" Kawabata pointed to the opposite wall where a large canvas was propped. A slash of burnt umber ran across a background of smoky gray, and three gouts of cerulean blue hovered in the upper right-hand corner. It was a bold, spare, somber, and illogical painting of such commanding presence that Boyle took his breath in with a hiss. The little artist, who smelled like a distillery, had created a powerful work. Now, like an idiot, he was bobbing his head in duck fashion, trying to elicit from his dealer a favorable response.

Before Boyle could think of anything to say, Mrs. Kawabata had thrust a glass of whiskey into his hand.

"Thank you," he said, ignoring the bobbing at his side.

They sat around the table and began to drink. Boyle relaxed as the couple talked in Japanese and the woman interpreted her husband's bland remarks. "Kenzo says he likes your tie." "Kenzo says you have lost weight." "Kenzo says you very handsome."

Finally Boyle said, "Tell Kenzo that's a good piece of work."

When this was related to the little man, he started to sing joyfully in a high wailing voice, swaying to the rhythm. The woman explained proudly that this was an old Japanese folk song popular at harvest time. Then she whisked Boyle's half-empty glass away and refilled it. Boyle sat back and drank, listening to the harsh, drunken voice. He felt at home, living a life appropriate for him. At last he got up and said good night, adding that Kenzo would have a show as soon as eight paintings were done; a spot would be kept open on the schedule. The last sight of the couple he had was of the little man bobbing his head obsequiously and the woman standing there serene and proud.

On the street, while pausing to absorb the luster of this interlude, Boyle noticed a man slipping around the corner, as if to avoid being seen. Had it been Vertrees? The man was tall and slim enough. But that was paranoia whispering again like Iago at his ear. Boyle hailed another taxi and stopped a block from his home, where in a grocery store he bought a dozen eggs, a pound of bacon, a loaf of French bread, a pint of chocolate ice cream. Before going home, he purchased two chilled bottles of California chablis at the neighborhood liquor store. He didn't know how he felt. The drinks had dulled his anxiety, but through his mind were whirling the faces of Victoria Welch and Cora and Warren Shore and Vertrees and Hopkins and then Tony Aiello slumped in blood against the warehouse and the white desert under a Utah sun and Julie Saunders naked among cushions. Was his life over? Kawabata's painting had renewed his desire for more of it. As he trudged up the stairs to his apartment, his mind settled on the image of Julie Saunders. After tomorrow, one way or another, he would be prevented from seeing her again. In his apartment he threw his shopping bag on the couch and dialed her number. It rang four times, so he hung up before the answering service informed him she was out. Wearily he slumped down beside the groceries and stared at his apartment; everywhere he looked he discovered things he loved—a painting, a sculpture, a piece of furniture. In his mood of heightened perception, he saw these things for what they were, the expression of his desire for peace and beauty. But there was another part of him that was still intensely alive. During the last week it had sustained him through two murders and the planning of fifty other deaths.

He got up and took the groceries into the kitchen. He was exhausted, slightly nauseated, and vaguely apprehensive. Twice today he had been wracked by sudden and unusual pain. It was, of course, gastritis, a chronic ailment brought on in the past by too much food and too many drinks. Or it could be a warning of what Victoria Welch, in her curiously moving way, had suggested. Certainly in recent days he had done everything possible to increase his cholesterol. Fat must be swimming in his blood, clogging the avenues of life. He slapped a dozen strips of bacon on a skillet and turned on a burner. The cosy sound of bacon sizzling filled the room. He broke four eggs cleanly with one hand and stirred them in a bowl along with some Tabasco and salt. A man under exceptional pressure could not be expected to follow a diet. In a pan he heated butter almost to burning and then dropped the eggs in. When the omelet was almost done, he folded it expertly with a spatula and slipped it onto a plate. He sprinkled parsley over the omelet and ate it and the bacon and the bread with glass after glass of chilled wine. He was on his last piece of bacon, when the doorbell rang. That could be Vertrees, he thought, and automatically touched the gun still in his gun holster. He could take it like the idealist Victoria Welch was or he could fight back like the professional he had always been. He walked toward the front door, extracting the Webley & Scott from the holster on his way. Right or wrong, he would go down fighting.

He flung open the door, stepped back to the side with the gun in his right hand, steadied by the left, and looked into the astonished eyes of Hirschorn.

"What the hell!" the pudgy man said and after a moment's hesitation brushed past the gun.

Quickly Boyle shoved it back into the holster, but stepped to the door and peered into the hall. Then he closed the door and walked into the living room, where Hirschorn was already sitting in a leather chair, eyes narrowed with both chagrin and amusement.

"Sorry," Boyle said.

"What in the hell was on your mind?"

"You know."

"No, I don't know."

"You know the situation I'm in."

"We're both in, Alex."

"I'm in. I'm the only one that woman knows."

"So?"

"So I'm the key."

"I agree you're the only one she knows."

Boyle sat down opposite the little man in the white shirt, dark suit, and conservative tie. It was somehow incongruous to be talking to Hirschorn about such matters; they should be discussing property taxes. "What's your own status?"

Hirschorn shrugged. "So far so good."

"I'm glad to hear that. I mean it."

"I know you do."

"Want a drink?"

Hirschorn waved his hand wearily. "No, I've had enough today."

"Me too, I'm afraid."

"So you're off your diet, huh?"

"Ho. Ho." Boyle pulled out his cigarettes and lit one.

"Better lay off those. When I talked to Hopkins just now, he said Spitz had gone into the hospital—lung cancer."

"That's rough."

"Well, I've known him for years." Hirschorn leaned back in the chair, looking smaller, as if the thought of Spitz had shrunken him. "Funny, isn't it, the way we get old?"

"Not so funny. You just talked to Hopkins?"

"Yes. Frankly, I don't think he's altogether happy with the decision."

"That sounds like good news for me."

"It is, Alex." Hirschorn smiled. "We're going to get you out of the country."

"Oh, you are?"

"You don't sound convinced."

"I'm not. Not with Vertrees breathing down my neck."

"*Vertrees?* You mean my son's friend?"

"Don't play games, Allen. We've known each other too long."

"I don't get you."

"You planted that kid in my gallery. Not that I blame you, but at least admit it."

Hirschorn shook his head slowly, his round, florid face sourly frowning. "You sound spooked."

Boyle stared and stared as if his eyes could verify what his mind would not: Hirschorn's deceit. A man never grew

175

wise in this business, Boyle thought. It was just possible that he, Alexander Boyle, a professional, was seeing trouble where there was none, an adversary in a friend, deceit in sympathy. "I guess I *am* spooked," he admitted gloomily. "I thought—well, let's forget what I thought."

"In your shoes I'd think the same thing. Only we'd both be wrong." Hirschorn spread his hands, palms up in a gesture of frustration. "How can I convince you? The truth is, some smart kids in Washington have come up with a good plan. It's so obvious we should have thought of it ourselves." Hirschorn grimaced. "Funny we didn't."

"Maybe it's old age," said Boyle. "So what's the idea?"

"Your driver and the librarian's nephew were working together."

"Well, that *is* a twist."

"And a good one. They robbed the bus and sent it over the cliff. You see, it's logical enough. Your driver had a long record, her nephew was a disturbed veteran."

That assumption had the clarity of a brash young man's logic. "So where do I come in?"

Hirschorn pulled out a long, black cigar, bit the end off meticulously, and struck a match slowly—a businessman's way of gaining time to think. "Alex," he said finally, blowing a decisive gust of smoke into the air, "you're going to be charged with killing them."

And then with increasing admiration for those "smart kids in Washington," Boyle listened to the realtor unfold the rest of the plan. Alexander Boyle, a former FBI agent and now an art dealer, had been involved in a heroin smuggling operation with Tony Aiello, a known criminal, and Warren Shore, a Vietnam returnee. When Boyle learned that they had been holding out on him, he tracked them down. This was the motive for the killings. It also provided the government with something to confess—a former agent had gone wrong—which would satisfy the blood lust of the public without doing irreparable harm to the bureau, especially because Boyle's records would be falsified to show that he had been fired for misconduct.

"It was a good move when you left heroin in the motel room," observed Hirschorn.

"It was merely procedure."

"Yes, but it's going to make things work. If we can brand the nephew a dope addict, we can handle the librarian. He gave her the stolen goods to hold, without telling her he killed a bunch of people to get them."

"But if he and Tony were dealing in big drugs, why would they attempt a cheap heist?"

"The smart kids in Washington have an answer for that. The dope was stashed on the bus. The robbery was just a cover-up."

"Would the kid keep the property, though? I mean, if he had a few kilos of heroin, he wouldn't bother keeping some watches and second-rate jewelry."

"That's a bit weak, I admit. And yet it's common knowledge that small-time drug peddlers don't give up *anything* of value. The kid might keep the stolen property for a rainy day. But because he'd double-crossed you, he had to get out of Frisco quick, so he left the stuff with his aunt along with a wild story about how he got it. Given her character, her kind of work, she'll come across looking pretty innocent."

"Huh," grunted Boyle.

"But it's logical, Alex. A little old librarian would defend her darling nephew. She wouldn't believe he was into drugs, much less cold-blooded murder, and she'd do anything to clear his name, even if she had to make wild accusations against the government. Alex, this woman is going to end up being a laughingstock."

"You don't know the woman."

"Believe me, this issue of drugs can ruin her credibility. How many families today appear on television, horrified to learn that sons and nephews have been dealing drugs and murdering people to do it?"

177

Boyle acknowledged the truth of that.

"Once we can explain the missing property, everything else falls into place. Defense and Agriculture both swear they've got control of the Baker station. Nobody there's going to open his mouth again. And as for the plane crash, that's easily explained—an act of God."

"It still sounds a little flimsy."

"But it can *work*. The key is linking you with those two and putting the whole affair down to a drug deal. Such schemes today are as common as pig tracks—at least in books and movies. And then to cap the whole thing, you bolt the country, disappear, a dishonored former servant of the United States Government."

Boyle lit a cigarette and puffed thoughtfully. "Well, it might work," he speculated after a while. "But the librarian won't give up easily."

"What can she do? There was heroin in the room where her nephew was killed. Army records show he'd made a poor psychological adjustment. Then a known hood was killed the preceding day by bullets from the same gun that killed her nephew. That's good circumstantial evidence of a link between the two. So the librarian takes a bus tour in a wild amateurish attempt to clear her nephew's name. She discovers in the newspaper that some employees of an agricultural station were killed in a plane crash. So what? She swears she met you, but you've flown the coop. Even if she had met you, what does that prove? Only that you were following her to recover the drugs you thought her nephew had left behind. In a few days the press will get the facts together, facts that make sense, and she'll be dropped like a hot potato. She might keep trying, but she'll be talking to the air. She'll be admired for her pluck, pitied for having such a nephew, and she'll be forgotten—just another fond relative of a kid gone bad."

Boyle could imagine her writing letters to Congressmen, demanding press interviews, exhibiting the foolish ardor of a childless woman who had poured all her maternal feelings into misguided love for a neurotic nephew. Days would lengthen into weeks and weeks into months as she bloodied herself against bureaucratic walls and endured the brutal rejection of reporters.

"She's quite a gal," Boyle murmured.

"And she's after your hide."

"Speaking of my hide, what did Hopkins want done?"

Hirschorn shrugged and searched for matches to relight his cigar.

"Did he want me hit?"

"You know as well as I do it was a possibility."

"Why didn't the people in Washington go along with him?"

"Thank your lucky stars for those smart kids in National Security. But you can't blame Hopkins for his opinion. It wasn't personal."

"No, probably not. He's for the simplest way. In his position I'd have the same idea." Boyle got slowly to his feet.

"We both would," said Hirschorn.

"How about some wine?" He went into the kitchen, got the half-empty bottle and two tumblers. "Here's to my new life," he declared, raising his glass to Hirschorn's.

"Where will you go, Alex?" And the realtor added quickly, "Better not tell me."

"When do you want me out of here?"

"By tomorrow night."

"That soon? Well, it's best." Boyle sipped the wine moodily. He pictured Cora packing their suitcases and saying, "I'm relieved, I'm relieved that you're out of it," and then he thought of Julie Saunders who would say nothing, but pack her suitcase as fast as she could. "Allen," Boyle said abruptly, "I may be taking someone along."

"A woman?" Hirschorn leaned forward when Boyle nodded. "Is that a good idea?"

"She won't be trouble. She won't ask questions."

179

"No? When it'll be in every paper?"

"She won't be trouble. I know what I'm doing."

"Maybe so, but I don't like the sound of it."

"Do me a favor, Allen. Don't mention this to Hopkins."

"I can't promise that."

"A favor for old-times' sake."

"Don't ask me." Hirschorn sat there blinking; then he intertwined his fingers and cracked his knuckles.

"I know what I'm doing. Do it for me, Allen."

Hirschorn pursed his lips as if tasting a lemon. "Damn you, Alex. We're acting like two old men, full of memories and sentiment. All right then," he said with a long sigh. "But I repeat—I don't like it. If the girl opens her mouth just *once*, you'll both get it."

"Allen. Thanks," Boyle said.

Hirschorn waved away the gratitude and hunched forward in the crisp attitude of a businessman closing a deal. "We better work fast. What name did you use on the last bank account?"

"T. A. Willis."

Hirschorn pulled out a spiral notebook and poised a pen over it. "That'll be your passport name." He looked up. "And your permanent name, Alex. We don't want federal agents tracking you down in a foreign country and extraditing you. What will the initials stand for?"

Boyle thought for a moment. "Thomas Albert." He didn't add that they were his grandfather's names.

"Okay. We'll transfer funds to that account first thing in the morning—registered, so you can withdraw them by noon. From what I understand, you'll have enough money for a year if you're careful. Is the girl's passport in order?"

"Knowing her," Boyle said, smiling, "I'm sure it is."

"What are you going to do about the gallery?"

Boyle poured another glass of wine, muttering, "Hell, I have shows scheduled for the next four months." For a moment he saw Kawabata staggering toward an immense white canvas, brush readied for the first thrust. "Allen, that gallery has got to keep going."

"You can't run it from where you'll be."

An odd and yet somehow fitting idea occurred to him. "What about turning it over to my assistant?"

"Well, it's legal enough," Hirschorn claimed. "But does he have the money to run it?"

"I'll leave him operating expenses for six months."

"Alex," said the realtor, "that's too much."

"He's still inexperienced. And I think women distract him. He may have a few setbacks."

"I'm not telling you what to do, but in your shoes I'd hold on to everything I had. Starting life in a new country isn't easy."

"Six months of operating expenses. Then it's up to him to make a go of it."

Hirschorn clapped the notebook shut. "That's your decision. But get this straight, Alex: When you leave, you're on your own for good." When Boyle nodded, the realtor planted his hands on his knees with finality. "Then that's that," he declared and got up with a sigh, as if he'd just made a bad deal. Boyle followed him to the foyer, where Hirschorn turned and said, "Give me your gun." He stretched out his hand. "That's evidence."

Boyle took the Webley & Scott from the holster and stared at the compact black shape that had been a warm, heavy sensation at his side for years. When he surrendered this gun, he left his life behind. After a short hesitation, he handed it to Hirschorn and opened the door. They shook hands without a word, then Hirschorn stepped into the hall. He turned suddenly, his face as unlined and pink as a child's. With a sidelong glance he mumbled, "Funny isn't it, I mean life," and moved rapidly toward the stairs.

The plan would work, if they effectively shackled Victoria Welch. That might prove far more difficult than the smart

181

kids in Washington claimed. If she persuaded a single reporter to take a hard look, a number of unsettling questions might arise. Had there, for example, actually been unusual experiments on a hog farm? Her activity could stimulate the demand for many clarifications. On the other hand, once this plan was set in motion, loose ends would tie themselves. It wouldn't be the first time during his years of service that Alexander Boyle had seen a flimsy idea evolve into a tightly structured operation. All that stood between the plan's inception and success was a lone woman who had worshipped her nephew. Boyle wanted her to fail. What could be gained for the country if she got her revenge? Her triumph would be abstract anyway, because the main object of her revenge would be thousands of miles out of the country. Would she find much satisfaction in avenging a dead boy at the expense of public trust in government? Well, perhaps she would; good people often found satisfaction in tearing down the system that protected them. And possibly her victory would mean the fall of a loyal man like Hirschorn. He was the logical choice to take the brunt, a man without official status who had endangered his life and reputation for a principle. Hirschorn must have realized his precarious position this evening. There went a real professional, wearing his dark suit, going home to a family every night, serving on civic boards, making his community a better place in which to live.

But for himself, Boyle thought, it was already all over. He had lost everything: reputation, vocation, and above all, the chance to live out his life in the country he had served so many years. And yet at least he could look forward to a new start, which was more than faced Victoria Welch if the plan worked. Of everyone involved, perhaps she would lose the most—her belief in justice. Idealists never win, Boyle thought, as he went for more wine. He poured it, noticing his hand tremble like an old man's. He had never felt so tired, so stunned by fatigue. He gulped down the wine,

182

hoping it would give him energy. Pouring another glass, he shuffled into the living room and flung himself on the couch. He felt as if he had walked miles. Then wearily he picked up the phone and called Julie Saunders, this time leaving a message with her answering service. "Tell Miss Saunders it's urgent," he said.

Then he sat back, waiting. What would she say to Hong Kong, New Delhi, Casablanca? He knew her. By noon tomorrow she would be ready to go, and he imagined them ascending the plane ramp like newlyweds, bound for anywhere. And yet he had no illusions. That girl, who hoarded things in her apartment like a chipmunk, would soon tire of a wandering life, assuming the money held out long enough for her to tire. She might then generously try for a while to look at him as someone different from what he probably was—the indulgent father she'd never had. But finally she would want something more than a dreary little life in Latin America or the Orient, where eventually he would have to settle as a shop clerk or bookkeeper, an aging expatriate steadily losing hope. He had no illusions. Their life together wouldn't last long, but for a little while they would sustain each other and be happy. That was enough.

He drank to the idea and stared lovingly at the possessions he would never see again. His had been a strange life, compounded of violence and beauty. He had seen blood spurting from the chest of a young man. He had seen a whole world created by a drunken artist. He had loved his wife. He had killed for his country. He had few regrets, no more probably than the average man who has made demands on people and acted at times callously. He had no regrets that would harass him in the future. He was sitting here waiting for the new life to begin with a short burst of happiness and to end years later in loneliness. With the melancholy anticipation of a man running off with a much younger woman, he was waiting for tomorrow.

He lifted his glass and toasted that tomorrow, feeling in

183

the next moment a pain of crushing immensity rivet him to the couch. He gasped for breath, as a hand inside of him remorselessly squeezed the air from his lungs. He could no longer avoid the truth. His body was suddenly a thing with a purpose of its own. He should call for help, but his fists wouldn't leave his chest; they stayed there as if trying to pry loose a stronger hand inside. This mustn't happen, this would complicate everything, he thought desperately, as the intensifying pain shot threads of itself from his heart to his shoulder, up to his teeth and down his left arm. Plans began to fade, the plans of Washington and Victoria Welch were fading, his own plan was fading too, his tomorrow was receding through the pain. This must not happen now, he told himself, and mouthed the words soundlessly, not now, not now, not now, until a white-hot crackling sensation swept through his brain like an enormous broom, and he jackknifed over.

Minutes later, when the phone rang, Alexander Boyle could no longer hear it. It rang and rang insistently. Then it stopped.